A modern-day and thought-provoking retelling of Oscar Wilde's *The Picture of Dorian Gray* that esteemed horror magazine *Fangoria* called "...a book that is brutally honest with its reader and doesn't flinch in the areas where Wilde had to look away.... A rarity: a really well-done update that's as good as its source material."

A beautiful young man bargains his soul away to remain young and handsome forever, while his holographic portrait mirrors his aging and decay and reflects every sin and each nightmarish step deeper into depravity... even cold-blooded murder. Prepare yourself for a compelling tour of the darkest sides of greed, lust, addiction, and violence.

I0590586

A FACE WITHOUT

A HEART

Rick R. Reed

A NineStar Press Publication

www.ninestarpress.com

A Face without a Heart

Printed in the USA

Print ISBN: 978-1-64890-023-5

NineStar Edition, June, 2020
Originally Published in 2000 by Design Image Group

Also available in eBook, ISBN: 978-1-64890-022-8

Warning: This book contains sexually explicit content, which may only be suitable for mature readers, graphic scenes of death, and use of narcotics.

For Nick and Sukie, each family in his own way

"If it were I who was to be always young, and the picture that was to grow old! For that—for that—I would give everything... I would give my soul for that!"

Oscar Wilde—*The Picture of Dorian Gray*

"Or are you like the painting of a sorrow,

A face without a heart?"

William Shakespeare—*Hamlet*

Prologue

GARY

There is blood on my hands. I look down at a body, a body that's become a thing—monstrous, ugly, inanimate. It could be a sculpture, a figure formed from wax or porcelain. The soul inside is gone, leaving a shell. I wipe a line of sweat from my forehead with a trembling hand, trying to tell myself these things, trying to believe that what lies at my feet is nothing more than an object, something to be reviled, something not worthy of further consideration.

It's not easy to believe. Although the corpse does not have a twinkle in its eye or the simple rise and fall of a chest, it's hard to remove myself from the plain fact that the body possessed those movements, those simple signs of life, just minutes ago. Distance, for now, seems more a matter of location than of feeling. The body at my feet wears the badges of its untimely demise—a dented face, a split-open skull, blood and grayish-pink matter seeping out. The bruises have already begun to rise, ugly yellow-pink things all over the body.

I stoop, plunge my fingers into the deepest hole, the one on the belly, to feel the warmth and the entrails. Amazed that the breathing has stopped. Amazed that I have such power.

I lift a finger to my mouth and slowly run it over my lips, the blackish liquid warm and viscous, metallic to the taste. I recall the vampire films I loved as a youth, never really believing such a thing could exist.

Now I do.

I have stolen a life so that my own might continue. There is something vampiric in that, isn't there? Because without this theft of a beating heart and an expanding and contracting pair of lungs, I would be unable to live.

Isn't that the real essence of the vampire?

It seems too quiet here, deep in the basement of a high-rise. A dull clanging is my only accompaniment, pipes bringing warmth and water to tenants above, whose lives continue, ignorant, untouched by my murderous hand. And that's the amazing thing, the thing that causes my breath, when drawn inward, to quiver.

Life goes on, in spite of this monumental act, just a quick, surprised scream and a heartbeat away.

There is blood on the walls, spattered Jackson Pollock-style. Who can say what is art and what is murder?

This so-called victim who now lies in final repose on a cold concrete floor, staring vacantly at nothing or perhaps at the hell that will one day consume me, can no longer chastise me, can no longer beg me to drop to my knees with him and pray, pray for forgiveness, imploring Jesus to lead me down the path of the righteous.

It's not too late, he said before I brought the mallet down on his skull, cracking it open like a walnut, slamming it into his windpipe, his gut, an eye socket, his shoulders as he fell, anywhere the mallet would ruin, destroying, sucking life.

He was wrong. The final irony of his existence, I suppose, is that he thought he had the power to do anything, to change another person, whom, I must admit, he cared very deeply about.

No, that power rests in my hand, the death-dealing claw that *changed* him. And people whine about how change never really lasts when it comes to others, how they always unfortunately revert to their old ways, the ways you don't want them to be. Anyone who has ever tried to change another knows this to be true. Oh certainly, the change may last a week, a month, even a year. But soon the real person comes back, the one who has been waiting in the wings for just the right cue, the one that will allow him to say "Ah fuck it, I've had enough."

But the change I've wrought in my friend can never be undone. He is dead and always will be. I have a power of which psychiatrists and psychologists can only dream. And I accomplished my transformation in a matter of seconds, behind a red-tinged curtain of rage.

Pretty sly, eh? For a man who's spent most of his life doing nothing but looking after his own selfish needs and pursuing his own pleasures, it's a pretty accomplished thing. Decisive. For once, a man of action.

I nudge him with my foot and am amazed at the heaviness my friend has taken on in death. His body doesn't want to give, to roll; it has become a body at rest...forever.

I turn and head back upstairs. There are matters to attend to...clothes to be burned, an alibi to be concocted. People will want answers. And conveniently, I will have none. Knowledge is a dangerous thing. What was it my other friend once told me? "The only people worth knowing are the ones who know everything and the ones who know nothing."

I know nothing about this. And now I must go back into the realm of the living to ensure my ignorance remains secure.

But alone, I know that ignorance is one of the few luxuries I can no longer afford. Alone, I have only the luxury of time to contemplate how it all began.

Book One

Chapter One

LIAM

He was beautiful. Beauty is so seldom ascribed to men, too often incorrectly attributed to men with feminine features—wavy blond hair, fine cheekbones, teeth cut from porcelain. But I've always thought of beauty as a quality that went deeper than the corporeal—something dark, dense, inexplicable, capable of stirring longings, primal longings one would be powerless to resist.

He was beautiful. I sat on a Red Line L train, headed downtown, bags of heavy camera equipment heaped at my side, one arm resting protectively over them. I watched the young man, unable to train my thoughts on anything other than this man who had blotted out the reality of the day, magical and transforming. Beauty, especially so rare a beauty, can do that. The young man was an eclipse, his presence coming between myself and the reality of the day hurtling by outside train windows.

He had come in behind three foreign people, a bright counterpoint to their drab colorless clothes which were already wilting in the August humidity. They chattered to one another in a language unrecognizable, Polish maybe, and I was annoyed at their yammering, unable to block it out sufficiently enough to concentrate on the book I was reading, a biography of William Blake.

I almost didn't notice him. It wasn't like me to pay much attention to what went on around me, especially when I was preparing for a shoot. Usually I used the time on the train to set up the photographs I would take, the way I would manipulate light and shadow and how it fell on my models, to arrange the props, set up and test the lighting.

But something caused me to look up when the doors opened—perhaps I was struck by the dissonance created by the unknown language—and I saw him. Close-cropped brown hair, a bit of stubble framing full lips, a bruise fading to dull below his right eye. The bruise did not detract from the man's beauty but served to enhance it, making of the rough features something more vulnerable. The bruise was the embodiment of a yearning for the touch of a finger, the whisper of a kiss. He wore an old, faded T-shirt with a Bulls logo, black denim cut off just above his knees, and a pair of work boots, the seam on the left beginning to separate. In spite of the workman's garb, there was something intellectual about the man, an intensity in his aquamarine eyes that portended deeper thought.

At that moment, I made a decision. I don't know what caprice seized me. I have always led an orderly life, completely without surprise. But when the train pulled to a stop and the young man stood, I acted on an impulse that was as sudden as it was uncontrollable.

I gathered my things together, stood, and hurried off the train. He was unaware that I was following. He traipsed down the stairs at the Belmont stop, summer light making slanted rectangles on the concrete floor of the station. Another L train rumbled overhead.

I watched him go through the turnstiles, then hurried outside into the heat, humidity, traffic, and voices raised above the hubbub. He had almost vanished into the crowd, but his beauty, a beacon, found me, and I stayed behind him, save for a few paces, unnoticed.

We walked for several blocks, east toward Lake Michigan. As we got off the more commercial boulevards and the storefronts gave way to apartment buildings fashioned from brick, from old gray stone, I trailed him down an alley.

He paused to light a cigarette. Even in this simple act, there was a quiet grace, a sureness of movement and purpose. He stood, exhaling, face obscured by a screen of pale gray smoke before the wind dispersed it.

I noticed suddenly we were alone. Things were quiet here in the heart of the North Side of the city. Insects chirped, and a breeze off the lake rustled the leaves. Rain had been promised for days, and perhaps the wind signaled its arrival.

Finally, almost alone with him in the alley, a beautiful young man and one older, laden down with heavy, awkward equipment and a completely illogical plan that was no plan at all... What would I do if he paused to ask what the hell I was doing? He remained, I think, blissfully unaware of my existence as he headed down the alleyway, stride purposeful.

I suddenly had a presentiment, and the feeling persisted—that of fear, a feeling that this young man held a sort of menace. I knew then he was a threat. All the sensible voices in my head formed a chorus, singing to me songs of urban tragedy, songs of pathetic older men lusting after younger ones. *Death in Venice*. This seemed to be a Midwestern sort of Tennessee Williams play, fraught with danger, bound to be wrapped up in disaster.

What if the man knew I was following and was leading me somewhere my screams wouldn't be heard? What if when we were alone, he would turn to me and, with the cunning smile of the serial killer, remove a knife from his work boot and spill my life all over the brick-cobbled streets? He would leave me, after slipping from me the burdens of my wallet and my camera equipment, my blood to drain into the bricks until some unsuspecting passerby spotted my prone form on the pavement and alerted the authorities. I could see it all, a Technicolor nightmare.

Photographers have visual imaginations like that. We have to; it's how we make our living.

I began to be seized with fear, a real, cold terror masquerading as common sense, that told me to get back on the train and on with my orderly life. But something made me press on, something in the sway of his hips as he walked quickly, heading farther and farther east as if he were a lemming and Lake Michigan's bouldered front his destination. His beauty made me feel I would follow him anywhere, even toward my own demise.

I had the sense he knew I was behind him. His steps slowed, faltered. I thought I could catch peripheral movement of his eyes as he strained to look behind him without turning his head.

He would be one of the young men, I thought, who enjoyed a good fag bashing, and this older man—only in my thirties, really, but already showing the signs, the thinning patch at the top of my head, fragile lines appearing around my mouth and on my forehead, strands of gray in my goatee—would make a perfect victim. After all, didn't I deserve to be punished for my inverted lust?

But on the train, I felt there was something different about this one. Even with that small glimpse, I knew the old clothes and the work boots were a lie. This man was made of finer stuff.

Still, I could be wrong. Chill fingers ran a glissando up and down my spine, playing the discs like piano keys.

He flicked his cigarette away, where it sparked and sent out a shower of ashes when it hit a brick wall.

And then he stopped. He turned to face me, and a smile played about his lips. His face was radiant! The smile served only to light up the perfect countenance, the fine cheekbones and perfect teeth, aquamarine eyes, a cleft in his chin—all these elements that came together to form something more ethereal. His beauty was difficult to describe in a language containing only twenty-six letters.

And it was his beauty that, for the moment, obliterated my fear and the good sense with which I lived my life. But I have lived with common sense for far too long to ignore it. I wanted to turn and run, and then the absurdity of the image assaulted me—a thin, balding man, running cockeyed down an alley, burdened with lenses, camera bodies, a tripod—all these things banging against me, weighing me down and making my movements leaden, like in a nightmare. With my handicap and his youth, he could have overtaken me in seconds.

So I stopped too and stupidly grinned.

He grinned back, and I wasn't sure if there wasn't a hint of menace in that grin, the cat toying with the mouse just before he pounced. I felt the chill again—a cold that emanated from within, having nothing to do with the hot, fetid breeze that blew through the trees above us. I pictured it all—the grin never leaving his perfect face, my mouth opened in a surprised *O*, the embodiment of Munch's *The Scream*. I would back from his smiling face, that evil, devilish grin, dropping my lenses, camera bodies...the tripod...stumble over them as he overtook me, as the sun moved into place behind him to cast a long shadow, to make of him a silhouette to my blinking eyes.

"What do you want?" There was no fear in his voice. If anything, there was only a hint of amusement in that musical inflection, deep, slightly scratchy. The grin continued, lessened but there, playful.

I bit my lower lip, not sure what I should say. What *could* I say? I didn't know myself what it was I wanted. A little voice inside me whispered with a deep, throaty laugh, "To have you invite me home, to let me worship you. No reciprocation needed. Just let me worship at the altar of your perfection."

I felt like a fool. Where was the self-esteem I had worked so hard to procure? Psychoanalysts and therapy groups, nothing more than wasted time and money.

"I... I..." Faltering, I stared, face burning, at the brick backs of the three flats that walled us in together, a sheet of newspaper rustling down the alley until a brown-painted dumpster arrested its flight.

The man shrugged, turned, and began to walk away, striding faster now.

I caught up, inspiration and desire mingling, a way to redeem myself.

I laid a hand on his shoulder. Beneath the thin cotton of his T-shirt, I felt the bone wrapped in muscle, silken skin. That small touch was electric. He stopped and turned once more to look at me.

"Yes?"

Stupidly, I smiled, fumbled for my wallet, withdrew a card. Liam Howard, Photographer. Custom Holograms. My address and phone number. I held the card out to him like a gift, its white glare trembling slightly.

He took the card and read it over.

"I'm Liam... Liam Howard," I stammered. "I'm a photographer." Of course I was! Wasn't that what the card I had just handed him said? When did I become so helpless, reduced to a tongue-tied adolescent under this god's aquamarine stare? But the truth was, and this is hard to believe, I was reduced by this beauty, a beauty unlike any I had ever seen. "I occasionally do exhibits," I blurted. "You know, my own stuff...at the galleries down in River North. I work with holograms...pretty exclusively. Not like the stuff you see in malls, but full three-dimensional images that I showcase in glass domes." I bit my lip and said it, feeling I had nothing to lose. "I'd like to make one of you. Do a portrait, you know? Have you ever done anything like that?"

He shook his head. "Not me." He stared at the card, almost as if there was something he had missed, probably looking for the con this odd man was trying to play. "What do you want in return? You want me to pay you or something?"

"No, no! I don't want anything from you but some of your time. Listen, I have a show opening Friday at the Ling Gallery, down on Superior. Come and see my work." I shrugged. "You'll see I'm legit, and you can get an idea of what I do."

He stood silently. I could imagine what he was feeling, that this had to be some sort of come-on and that he would be better off to turn and go home before this ruse went any further.

"I could pay you, if that's what you want."

I was about to offer him $100 an hour, but before I could, he said, "It might be fun. Sure, I'll do it."

"Do what? Come to the opening or pose for me?"

"I'll come to the opening. We can go from there."

"What's your name?"

He smiled, and again I felt an electric surge.

"Gary," he said, extending a large hand. "Gary Adrion."

Chapter Two

GARY

West Superior, I suppose, has become the SoHo of Chicago, in spite of the South Loop renaissance and the desire of developers to have it known as SoLo. West Superior and the streets running parallel to it have become known, in the past several years, as River North. These streets are filled with Chicago's sensible brick buildings, once home to industry and offices, now converted into lofts and gallery after gallery after gallery. Loft or gallery, the gentrification of this area makes for a couple of common traits. The spaces have become filled with the young, professional, and affluent...who, in reality, are yuppies but think they are too hip to be saddled with such a clichéd moniker, and decor which, whether home or business, leans toward a lot of stark white and exposed brick walls, hardwood floors, and recessed lighting.

I have always been a lover of art. I grew up around it. My grandfather, who, at least in name, raised me, covered our North Shore walls with the best of the French impressionists. I sometimes thought he was trying to compete with the Art Institute's collection. Our walls featured Degas, Cezanne, Monet, Manet...enough to warrant a whole stronghold of security systems and alarms.

My own tastes have come to run afoul of my grandfather's, and although I haven't yet been able to become the kind of collector he was, I am the proud owner of a Hockney and two Keith Harings.

When Liam Howard invited me to his opening, he probably didn't realize I would be on familiar ground. Not the day I met him, anyway, when I was got up in working class garb. I must have looked like rough trade. But this rough trade is neither rough nor trade. I would never mention it to Mr. Howard, who seems in all respects a gentleman of the old school, but to be perfectly hateful, yet honest, I have come to inspire the attentions of aging queens like himself since I was about fourteen years old.

But his interest in creating holograms as a sort of new art form intrigues me. I had once been to the Salvador Dali museum in St. Petersburg, Florida, where I saw a haunting hologram of, believe it or not, the rock musician Alice Cooper. The miniature ephemeral Cooper stuck with me, but I had yet to see any other artists who used this medium. I would say that all I had seen had been abused, the carnival-like "art" of the shopping mall, attention-getting packaging and lurid buttons dragging this art form down to the gauche.

The Friday night of Liam's opening is a rainy one. August. The air cloaked with a misty rain and humidity so thick you can almost touch it. I am dressed a little more refined but not much—a black T-shirt and a pair of SilverTab Levi's, with the requisite chain dangling from my right hip, attached to my wallet. A pair of black Sketchers. Trip-hop, I guess you'd call it, and I pray Liam Howard, who is beyond the age of such wear, will not try to dress the same. I want to like him, and if I see him dressed in clothes that are too young for him, well, it will alter my good first impression of him pretty seriously.

I mount the stairs of the Ling Gallery and push through heavy glass doors. I don't see Liam immediately. The place has filled in pretty well. Old Mr. Howard must do all right for himself. The crowd is peppered with young people dressed in similar fashion to mine, the Goth crowd in their heavy makeup and black everything, and the middle-aged, "hip" suburbanites who come in from the North Shore, attired also in black, but theirs is Donna Karan, Vera Wang, and Versace, as opposed to the thrift store jumble favored by the Goths.

There is, of course, the requisite white-linen-topped table near the front, with an open guest book and a pen. Bottles of Pellegrino are lined up on its surface, along with a plate of Brie, white grapes, and French bread cut in slices. Beer and wine are available for four dollars in little plastic cups. Near the table is a sign, hand lettered, on an easel. The sign reads *Liam Howard. Holographic Hallucinations*.

I pass, shutting out the voices and the stares, and begin to mill around the lofty, open space. I want to see Liam Howard's art, see it alone. I have always had the ability, when around true art, to tune out the background static and tune in to it. I guess you could say this is one way I define good art. It lets me bring it to the forefront, no, *forces* me to bring it to the forefront, while all around me becomes a sort of white noise.

What Liam does with his art takes me away. Once I start looking, the people around me, their conversation and laughter, their faces and expressions and how they mill, swarm around the exhibit, all vanish.

I will admit, it isn't just the execution—although as you will see, that word is a bit of a pun—of his art that transfixes me, but the subject matter itself.

Liam is fascinated with the bizarre, with death, with violence. Such a contrast to the man I had met the other day! How such lurid visions could come from the psyche of such a...well, such a milquetoast, is both jarring and, in its own way, delightful.

His vision is disturbing, though, and I'm sure that's the word reviewers use most often when they write about his work, even though I've never seen a single review. That word can encompass all that's good about his work as well as, for those who aren't enlightened enough to appreciate it, panning him.

Some of the holograms remind me of the work of the photographer Diane Arbus. These are people on the fringe—dwarves, a circus Fat Lady, nude, her corpulent rolls seeming to slide off her body, a stripper in tasseled pasties and G-string.

All the holograms are encased in cylinders of glass. They move when one walks around the circumference of the glass. For example, the Fat Lady lifts an éclair to her mouth continually, for as long as one cares to encircle the piece. I suppose there is a statement in the infinity of this action.

All of them have a ghostly quality. The images are transparent, seemingly crafted from light (which, I suppose, they are) that gives them a phosphorescence, a glow that makes them otherworldly. They are almost too real, as if these are not holograms but actual miniature people trapped inside glass.

And then there are the more violent visions, stark and frightening. Here is the man in the claw-footed tub. As I make my journey around him, he lifts a straight razor to his wrist and slashes. Walk a little farther and his image disappears into the tub. Here are the two lovers embracing, she a long-limbed black girl with dreadlocks and he a body builder with a blond flattop. Their caress turns to strangling as I make my circular route around the piece. Here is the flaxen-haired waif, who couldn't be more than fourteen, shooting up.

It's almost too much. I feel jarred when the voices and bodies around me suddenly come back, as if I've been in some sort of fugue.

I have yet to see Liam, and I wonder if he has defied convention and not turned up.

It doesn't matter. I can't get these images out of my head, and I need air. I jostle my way through the crowd and head outside, where twilight has come. Steam rises off the hot concrete. The rain has stopped.

It will be interesting to see what Mr. Howard does with *my* image.

Chapter Three

HENRIETTA

"I just don't know how I'm gonna stand this fuckin' gig any longer! That manager is going to drive me insane. I swear on a stack of Bibles!"

I paced the plank flooring of Liam's studio, sucking a cheroot down in a couple of puffs. Liam had some new-age crap on the CD player, and it was righteously irritating me.

"What is this? Sounds like elevator music!" I crossed to the CD player, and before Liam could begin to say Vangelis, I had ejected the cartridge and was already rifling through it to find the offending disc. "I don't know how you get any work done, listening to this shit. Music soothes the savage breast, honey, but this is ridiculous."

I pulled out the disc and stomped on it with a red spike heel, custom-made for the purpose of murdering bad music. I stooped to where he had countless CDs stacked on the floor of his loft. I pulled out one that was halfway decent, one I was surprised old Liam would even own. Some fuckin' model must have left it here. I put it back in the CD player and pressed Play.

Lighting another cheroot, I exhaled and said, "Much better," as Moby filled the big space. "You of all people, L, should know that bad music is not to be tolerated. It'll rot your soul, baby. Now where was I? Oh yeah, this goddamn asshole down at the club... He's not up for givin' me a raise. I been shakin' my ass there for two years, drawing a bigger and bigger crowd all in the interest of makin' his scrawny white ass rich, and he tells me he can't afford it. Shit."

I stopped and looked at Liam. The guy and I had been friends for years. A more unlikely twosome could not be imagined, but I loved Liam like family. Five years ago he had come to watch me in some wood-paneled dive on the South Side, and of course he was enchanted with Lady Henrietta Wotton's spell. This girl can sing, no lip-synching for me, uh-uh. He came up to me after the show like some nervous suitor, wearing a fuckin' suit, of all things. Tells me he wants to make a hologram of me. A hologram, honey! Can you imagine! A little doll-sized Henrietta under glass...kinda makes you think of that doll that scared the shit out of Karen Black in *Trilogy of Terror*, that old TV movie schlock-fest. The rest, as they say, is history. A picture of that very same hologram appeared on the cover of *Chicago* magazine, and when everyone was lining up to see it and some of Liam's other, I must admit, *bizarre* work, both our fortunes took an upward turn.

"Why don't you get out, then?" Liam asked, perfectly reasonably. "I'm sure you must have had other offers."

"Oh sure, they're just beatin' down the door for drag queens. Where am I gonna go, the Baton?"

Liam rolled his eyes. He knew me well enough to know that when I was on a rampage, there was no reasoning with me.

Suddenly, I was tired of bitching. A first for me, but the day and the music just made me want to push all the hatefulness away. It was poisoning nobody's heart but my own. Three days ago the rains came, and they finally made at least a few days of this summer bearable. Finally there was a little relief from that pancake-melting, mascara-running humidity. I moved to the beat of the song, "Feeling So Real," and just let Liam watch me. That's kind of what our relationship has been based on, me the performer and Liam the audience. It worked out. It always has.

I stopped and shook another cheroot out of the pack. I knew I should throw that dog a bone. "So, what have you been working on? Run across any beautiful boys lately?"

Liam was bent over a long wooden worktable, scarred. It must have been a hundred years old. He stood up.

"As a matter of fact, I have."

I winked. "Uh-huh. You can tell Henrietta. What happened?"

"Nothing like that."

Liam's face gets all pinched when he's outraged. It was really kind of cute, but I wouldn't tell him that.

"This young man has the most incredible beauty I have ever seen. I mean it. He is an Adonis... perfect." Liam paused to look outside at the bright blue sky, almost as if he was searching for just the right word, written there on the clouds. "His beauty is... absolutely incorruptible."

"Honey, there ain't no such thing. I never met a man can't be corrupted." I leaned up close to him. "And I don't want to."

"Well, let's see what you think when you see what I've done with him. I think it's the finest work I've ever done." Liam looked down at the floor for a minute, frowning. "I wish I could say it was due to my artistry, but I can't. This boy, Gary, is the kind of subject photographers can only dream of. You just step back and record it."

"Well, let's see! Let's see! Don't *even* tell me you haven't finished it yet."

"Oh, it's finished. After he was here for his session, I was up all night..."

"Uh-huh." I laughed.

"Nothing like that!" Liam said, offense showing around the thin lines creasing his mouth. "I was up all night *working*. I had to see if the result would be as good as I expected."

"And was it?"

"It was better."

"I suppose you'll put it in your next show." I swear on a stack of Bibles, as soon as the words were out of my mouth, my friend's expression changed to... What was it? Fear?

"I don't know if I'll exhibit this one."

"Why the hell not? You said it was your best work."

Liam moved away from me and busied himself at the damn table again, taking up his letter opener and going through bills. Lady Henrietta has never been one to be ignored. I grabbed his hand and took the letter opener and a bill, set them back down on the table.

"Why not, Liam?"

He wouldn't look at me. "It's a long story."

He wouldn't say any more, so I asked, "You gonna let me see this masterpiece or not?"

"Gary's coming over this afternoon. I want him to be the first." Liam allowed himself a small smile. "He should be the first for the...unveiling."

"Liam! Liam, Liam. You should know you can't treat me like this." I was beginning to get just a little impatient. His reticence was working my nerves, and I was in too good a mood for that.

"The truth is, Henrietta..." Liam gave me a small, embarrassed smile. "The reason I'm reluctant for anyone to see the portrait is that maybe my work was too good."

"Go on." Sometimes I just did not understand this man.

"It all shows. It all shows."

"What are you talking about?"

Liam threw up his hands, as if he were helpless. Liam is a lot of things, but underneath that timid façade, he is not helpless. At least not until today.

"I worship this guy." He paused to take in a breath. "I'm in love with him, Henrietta, and I might as well have just written it across the hologram... you know, a kind of neon heart above his image. It shows so plainly there."

"And what, pray tell, is wrong with that? I've found new love to be one of the most charming of emotions." I snickered. "Pity it never lasts."

"Don't be so cynical! Don't you believe in true love?"

"Honey, I believe in three things—money, pleasure, and freedom. In that order. There's no such thing as true love... You just got the hots for this stud."

Liam shook his head as if he pitied me. But I had no time for pity.

"How will you ever be happy with a view like that?"

"Happiness is for the dull... They think it's like some destination you reach, and once you get there, you're set. I'm just realistic, sweetie. You grab happiness when it comes along, gobble it up, and if you're lucky, it stays with you for a while. As far as true love, it doesn't exist. The hots exist, and I think that's what you feel for this... What did you say his name was? Gary. That's why love never, ever lasts. Nothing does. This isn't a permanent world."

"So nothing lasts?"

"Nothing, honey. Even this boy's good looks... They'll leave him one day, and he'll just be another tired old man, lusting after a young one, whatever spins his top. Good thing he at least had an artist like you to get it all down."

"Well, if I may say so, I've done an admirable job of capturing his radiance."

"God! You talk like a book. So, are you going to let me see it or not?"

"Not. Now Gary will be here soon, and there's no way I'm scaring him off with the likes of you."

"Is Lady Henrietta being ejected from the premises?"

"Exactly."

I pretended to be huffy. Pretending or real, nobody but me knows for sure. And unfortunately, Liam. I dropped the front. "Oh come on, baby, let me hang around and meet this god."

"Absolutely not."

"Wait a minute! What did you say this character's name was? Gary? He's not Gary Adrion by any fat chance?"

Lord, you'd think I had hauled off and slapped Liam across the face.

"You know him?"

"I know of him. The manager"—I loaded my voice up with sarcasm on *that* word—"is putting together this AIDS fund-raiser for Labor Day weekend, a big dance party with all the pretty boys at the Uptown Theatre, and he mentioned the name. Said he's helping with the setup."

Liam looked horrified. "He's involved with that?"

"Honey, don't look so *disturbed*. He said he was glad he found this kid, a straight guy, not into the bar scene at all...because he was so, so passionate about helping people. He does whatever Bill tells him. More than I can say for moi!"

The relief that softened Liam's features was immediately apparent.

I waved my hand. "I wish I had asked to meet him at the time. Had I known he was your latest *crush*..."

"It's nothing like that..." Liam sighed.

"I would have insisted on getting a gander myself."

We paused as the buzzer sounded, an electronic buzzing like some giant insect. I grinned, cocked my head. "I think that just might be your Mr. Gary Adrion."

"Damn!" Liam whispered, hurrying to the intercom on the opposite wall.

I could only grin.

Chapter Four

GARY

I hear the music from all the way downstairs...a thumping dance beat, something industrial. This surprises me because it isn't what I expect from Liam, who has seemed somewhat, well, reserved. When I posed for him a few days earlier, the music had been mellow, stuff like Dead Can Dance, Deep Forest, Hildegarde Von Bingen. There is an atmosphere of calm in his studio, and I can't imagine the mood that has seized my new friend.

Liam opens the door, and the studio seems a different place, alive with the day's summer light and the pulse of the music's bass line. It puts me in a happy mood. I'm eager to see the hologram. We had done hours of shooting, from every conceivable angle, and I had no idea how these images would look in the final analysis. What would I be doing? I mean, would there be movement incorporated into the final image? Would I be smiling? Somber? Standing or reclining? Both?

Before I have a chance to dwell much more on what I am about to see, a door at the back of the studio creaks open, and emerging from it is one of the most beautiful women I have ever seen. A black woman, dressed in red crepe de chine with red high heels to match. There is something about the style of this woman that seems both glamorous and false. Her skin is that smooth café au lait you sometimes see in Creole women in New Orleans. Her makeup is heavy—false eyelashes, blusher, eyeliner pulled into a Cleopatra-like upsweep at the corners of wide golden eyes. And yet it all seems natural. She smiles, revealing perfect white teeth, save for a thin gap in the middle that reminds me of the model Lauren Hutton. She holds forth a large hand, capped with blood-red nails so long they curve a bit at the ends.

"You must be Mr. Adrion."

Her voice is husky, and when she grips my hand, it's with surprising strength. As I shake it I realize suddenly that beneath this veneer of feminine charm, a man is hiding. I don't know what kind of man, because my experience with this sort of thing is limited, but a man nonetheless.

She catches my stare, and I realize she knows what I'm thinking.

"Oh, Liam, this one here is perceptive. Sees right through Miss Henrietta."

Her golden eyes flash on mine.

"It's all about illusion, honey. You remember that."

I don't know what to say or feel. Embarrassment? Relief that I don't have to play along with the ruse? Her smile calms me, almost as if she is glad we're in on her little secret. I say "she" because, in spite of the sudden knowledge of her true gender, the femininity she projects far outweighs the scared little man I know is hiding behind the front.

I say nothing, even though the truth resides in our glances. "I'm pleased to meet you. What did you say your name was? Henrietta?"

"*Lady* Henrietta Wotton, thank you very much. I believe you know the manager of the shithole, excuse me, *establishment*, where I ply my trade."

I cock my head.

"Bill Kross—or Auntie Bee as we call her—the owner of the Façade, down on Rush Street."

I nod. I've been working with the man on setting up a party for an AIDS benefit for the upcoming Labor Day weekend. I had seen a sign for the benefit a few weeks ago that said they were looking for volunteers. Out of boredom and, yes, a desire to do something for the good, I called him.

"He's a good man. I believe in what he's doing." I smile and almost wither under the glare that suddenly creases her features.

"He's an asshole," Henrietta hisses. "His benefits make him a ton of money. Don't you kid yourself, sweetie."

Liam stops her. "Now, that'll be quite enough, Henrietta. Don't go poisoning the boy with your bile."

Henrietta grins and winks, making us conspirators. As if she is saying *Humor him. We know the truth, don't we?*

I turn to Liam, breaking the spell Henrietta seems willing to cast all day long with her gaze. "So, is it ready? I was thinking about it in the cab on the way over here, and I can't wait to see it. I mentioned your work to a couple of people, and they were impressed that I was posing for you."

Liam stares at the floor, face reddening a bit. "I just have a few finishing touches...technical stuff, you know. Then I'll put it in its dome and *voilà*... It'll be art." He smiles. "And then we can have the unveiling. I wanted it to be just you and me, but Henrietta here insisted on staying."

"That's right, honey. No one can resist this girl's charms."

Liam shakes his head, and I laugh.

"I wouldn't want it any other way."

Henrietta takes my arm.

"I like this boy. I can see why you're so taken with him, Liam."

"Henrietta," Liam warns.

"Why don't I fix Gary and me a couple of cocktails, and we'll retire to the terrace while you finish up with your masterpiece?"

Liam frowns, but he says, "That sounds like a splendid idea."

*

Outside, the day is warm with a hint of breeze moving across the tops of the buildings. The air is crisp and not weighed down with the humidity that has plagued the city all summer. Henrietta, of course, would never settle for a couple of beers. She's mixing up martinis in the corner of Liam's terrace, Gilbey's and a silver shaker, those elegant glasses.

She finishes and brings me mine. I sip and hate it but try not to let it show.

"Good, huh?"

She winks. I wonder if she can read my mind. I laugh.

"Martinis are one of the last bastions of the civilized man. You should learn to like them."

"Mmmm." I sip again and try to appreciate the cold liquor sliding down my throat. "It's beautiful up here, isn't it?" We both look at the view from Liam's rooftop terrace. To the east, Lake Michigan is a roiling aqua expanse, and to the south, the skyline of the city rises up, the towers imposing, breathless, a wonder that seems more a force of nature than something man-made.

"We've got it all right here, don't we, handsome?" Henrietta says.

"It is beautiful."

"More than beautiful, although I think beauty is far too maligned these days. It is one of the few things that make this life bearable. People want to trivialize it."

"Well, there are more important things."

Henrietta looks shocked. "Like what?"

I take another sip, beginning to appreciate the charm of a chilled martini in the heat of a summer afternoon. "Oh, kindness, compassion, hope, love..."

Henrietta shakes her head. Her shoulder-length black hair moves in the breeze. "All of it temporary, just like beauty. Beauty's the only thing we can appreciate with our eyes...reach out and touch it..."

And with this, she lays a gentle hand on my cheek.

"Those other things are just made-up concepts, probably by some fool trying to make himself feel better."

"Liam was right about you," I said, smiling, "You are cynical."

Henrietta frowns.

"But charming too! Don't ever forget that."

Henrietta's frown vanishes. "I just say what I think, honey. So few people do. And what I think is that all we can hold on to in this world is what we can see and touch...not what some asshole tries to make real by putting some words behind it. I read somewhere once that this is one of the great secrets of life—'To cure the soul by means of the senses and the senses by means of the soul.'"

I cock my head, not sure what she means. She laughs at me.

"You look like one of those little dogs, cocking your head 'cause you don't understand. You will one day, trust me—you will. Right now, in that pretty face, you know more than you'll ever need."

We stop when the terrace door creaks open. Liam stands there, a pale figure on the threshold, darkness gathering behind him.

"It's ready."

He turns, and we set down our drinks and follow. I feel a breathless rush, more than I expected, as if this unveiling will mark some sort of change in my life, as if a new chapter is being opened...and I wonder what dark tale this chapter will be part of. I shake my head, thinking this is my vanity taking over, giving a momentousness to the occasion that it doesn't deserve. I also think how Henrietta would disagree, how she would tell me my youth and good looks are the only thing I have. A depressing thought, but she wouldn't agree with that assessment.

The studio feels cool after the sun outside. It's hard to see because my eyes haven't adjusted yet.

But I can see the black rectangle topped with a glass dome and the play of light inside. There is a curious moment, just a moment, though, when I feel I might be better off just not looking at it. As if seeing myself captured in this way will somehow change the course of things.

Oh come on now, Gary.

Henrietta stands in front of the glass dome, biting on one of her nails. It bothers me a little that she's not saying anything. Even though I just met her, I know for sure that there are not many times when she doesn't have anything to say. I wonder if her silence is due to disappointment or awe.

I walk up behind her and stop. Henrietta's dark hair blots out the image, and again I feel as if I might be better off if I just don't look. *Why am I feeling like this? On the way over, I couldn't wait to see what Liam had done.*

Henrietta reaches back and grabs my hand, squeezes and lets go. I close my eyes, listening to the click of high heels on hardwood.

I open my eyes, and for a moment, everything seems unreal. It's a dream. That's all. A dream. I had, of course, seen myself on video. Who hasn't? But this was different. This, this...*piece* has an otherworld quality, something so strange and magnificent that my eyes well with tears. There I am...captured forever in a faint pinkish glow. I had posed naked for Liam, knowing he was attracted by my body but that his real passion lay in his work.

And now it shows. I bite my lip, a strangled sob in my throat. Am I really that beautiful? Oh God, that sounds so vain! But you have to understand. What Liam has done seems too good to be true. He has taken everything good about me and elevated it somehow. That has to be it, of course. My image stands in the middle of the glass dome, as if I'm trapped inside and staring out. As I travel around its circumference, the image raises his arms, the muscles bunching and lengthening under the phosphorescent skin. There's a perfectly flat stomach, the abdominals clearly defined. My hair, stubbly yet thick, almost begs to be touched.

God, will I ever be this young again? Will I look like this next year? The year after? I understand now what Narcissus felt when he gazed into the pool. I hate myself for being so vain...and try to ascribe the beauty of this portrait to Liam's hands.

"God!" I gasp. "It's really flattering."

"No," Liam says. "It's not flattering. It's you."

My skin is touched with a faint veneer of sweat, making it shine, giving it a texture that makes you want to touch. My eyes seem to reach out, alive, from the hologram, to engage.

I feel almost sick. How dare I think so much of myself? But the hologram is stunning, breathtaking. It's depressing, though, to think that, even if this is really what others see when they look at me, this beauty is nothing I can hold on to, nothing that won't wither on the vine, darken, age... This beauty is nothing like a quick wit or a keen intellect, qualities that can be improved by age and the acquisition of wisdom... It's temporal. And it frightens me to think that this could be the very best of me. What will I do when it's gone?

"Damn," Henrietta whispers, "you are one gorgeous man."

I shake my head, staring at the strong form, the defined muscle, the face that looks carved from marble. Suddenly I feel sad. I think of how Henrietta and I talked of beauty on the rooftop, and I think how it isn't fair that even now, this beauty is slipping away, moment by moment.

"What's the matter, Gary?" Liam puts a hand on my shoulder. "Don't you like it?"

"Oh, that's not it. I... I love it."

"It's my masterpiece, you know. I know that sounds pretentious, but it's the finest work I've ever done."

"I do believe you're right, Mr. Howard. Even better than me, and honey, that's saying a lot." Henrietta moves closer to me. "Look at you. A finer specimen has not been created."

"And that's just the problem," I whisper, turning away from the portrait, tearing myself away, actually, because I think I could look at it all day. "You were right, Henrietta. Youth and beauty are more important than we give them credit for."

"Anyone says different is just paying lip service."

I shake my head slowly, returning my gaze to the portrait. "Damn. I'd give my soul to always look like that." A short, humorless laugh escapes me, almost choked out by despair. "Why can't it be me who will always look like that and the hologram that would age?" The flawless eyes stare back. "Sign me up, Devil. I'll give you my soul..."

"Don't talk like that!" Liam snaps.

"Hush," Henrietta says, lighting a cheroot. "Boy's got the right idea."

Liam moves slowly to the table and rummages, emerging at last with a hammer. "Gary, if it bothers you that much, I'll pound it to pieces."

"Liam!" Henrietta gasps.

"I don't want anyone selling his soul to the devil over my work."

I take the hammer from Liam's hand, and for a moment, we touch. The feel of skin against skin is electric, and our eyes meet and lock for a moment. "It's your masterpiece," I say softly. "Don't be ridiculous." I place the hammer on the table.

There is little more to say. The anticipation over, the room suddenly seems a void, a vacuum. As if taking this moment for a cue, Henrietta turns to the door.

"I have to be leaving now, boys. Lots for me to do to look beautiful for tonight's show." She catches my eye. "Unlike you, Gary, this girl's got to work to shine." She starts toward the door, opens it, and pauses. "Say, honey, why don't you come by the club tonight? You could catch my act, and we could grab a couple of 'tinis afterwards and get better acquainted."

I smile. "I'm not doing anything tonight. That sounds like a great idea."

"I begin at midnight." With that she walks quickly over to Liam and me, pecks us on the cheeks, and before we have a chance to say anything, she is gone, the door closing behind her, the clatter of her high heels down the stairs a diminishing echo.

I turn back toward Liam. "Thank you. It really is something. Can I take it now?"

"It's all yours."

Liam's eyes seem to get larger and moisten. He busies himself boxing up the equipment I will need to display his work, putting things into boxes, stacking them, and tying them together with twine so it will be easier for me in the cab. I feel that, even though the hologram has been winked out for transport, the little man inside the glass dome still exists, as if he has taken on a life of his own. The idea makes me shiver.

"Will I be seeing you tonight at the Façade?"

Liam grins, but there is no mirth in it. "I'm afraid that such places are off limits for me. Never could stand the smoke, the crowd." He pauses. "Say, why don't you skip that whole thing tonight, and you and I will go to dinner. My treat."

"Liam, I already promised Henrietta..."

Liam waves his hand. "Henrietta is the kind of person who likes one better if one breaks his promises. She sees it as a kind of moral fortitude."

"Well, I can't. But maybe another night."

"Count on it."

I make my exit. Just as I am about to go through the door, I take a look back at Liam. He is standing in the sunlight coming from the skylight above, but the light doesn't seem to penetrate him. He draws the shadows to him like a magnet, and there is something dark about him. He looks sad, and suddenly I don't want to take the time to try to figure out why.

Chapter Five

HENRIETTA

"I swear on a stack of Bibles, somebody swiped my eyeliner!" Honest to God, you couldn't trust one of these bitches alone with your things. I looked once more around the dressing room table, searching for the little red tube of liquid eyeliner that I had paid a king's ransom for just the week before. Gone. Fuck.

Stealing was only wrong when you're the victim. I waltzed over to Alotta Myles's, alias Kevin Small's, vanity and took her eyeliner, lining it up with the rows of cosmetics on the table in front of me. Honey, what goes around comes around.

I looked at myself in the dressing room mirror. A sallow black man with nappy hair and large eyes stared back. Lord, if these people ever got a load of me out of drag, they'd never believe it. I was never recognized if I ventured out as a man. Not that that's something I did with any frequency.

Outside, in the club, some Janet Jackson number with a heavy bass beat was drumming, vibrating the floors and putting me in a mood. Tonight I was nervous. Little secret, Miss Henrietta hardly ever gets nervous, but the presence of that boy, Gary, was giving me butterflies. Truth to tell, it was kind of a good feeling; took me back to my youth. I began applying my eyeliner, heavy black strokes artfully framing my "limpid pools." Hah!

Auntie Bee came into the dressing room. Or should I say squeezed into the dressing room, because Auntie Bee is getting bigger by the minute, I swear. Tonight he wore some gauzy caftan, no makeup, and his balding head was exposed for all the world to gawk at. Not a pretty sight, but one I've gotten used to.

"Great crowd out there tonight."

"So what else is new?" I began lining my lips in dark brown, making a perfect outline I'd fill in later with a rich shade of russet. "Honey, this place is crowded every night." The Façade had become Chicago's premiere drag club, eclipsing even the perennial Baton Show Lounge downtown. The difference lay in the simple fact that Auntie Bee provided a great dance floor and one of the hottest DJs in town, Tony Ricardo, so people could do more than just come here to watch the show.

Auntie Bee came up behind me and began massaging my shoulders.

"I hope this little act of kindness has everything to do with the fact that you're about to tell me you've relented on the raise issue."

Auntie Bee stopped kneading and caught my eye in the mirror. "Now, Hen, we've already been through this."

"Shit!" I flung the blusher brush to the table's laminate surface. "I work hard for you, motherfucker! I'm the reason this club has taken off, and you know it."

Auntie Bee shook his head. "Girl, you're getting yourself all into a fit. Muscles like steel under there. Don't tell me you're so tense because of the raise thing." He paused, and a small grin crept over his withered features. Thrice weekly visits to a tanning salon over the past five years will do that. "You'll get what you wanted... You just have to be patient for a little while is all. I'm still trying to get ahead. Things haven't been prosperous for that long."

"Don't give me that bullshit." I knew he was telling the truth, but I wasn't about to give him the satisfaction of calming me.

"Now, tell your auntie. Why are you so uptight?"

I thought how I should just get on with my transformation and ignore the little weasel, but I relented. "Got a special man in the house tonight, sweetie, and he's makin' me scared."

"Someone new in Henrietta's life?"

"Nothing like that, now. You know how Henrietta feels about love." I struggled into the nylon cap that would flatten my hair before I put my wig on. "You know the guy anyway. Gary Adrion?"

Auntie nodded. "Oh yes, I've known that boy's family for years. But don't you go telling him that. Don't want to reveal Auntie's dark past."

Everyone around the club knew Bill grew up privileged in Kenilworth, one of the richest suburbs in the United States. But in this environment, Bill had decided his past should be kept discreet. I don't blame him, considering the fact that his family threw his ass out going on more than twenty years ago now. If I ever met someone who's *not* from a dysfunctional family, I would have a coronary thrombosis, I swear. I picked up my wig, the straight black number, and began to brush it out. "So tell Henrietta the dirt on this boy. Maybe it'll relax me."

Bill's was a tale we had all grown to know. We had heard the story so many times. Sad little boy wants to be a girl. Invariably, sad little boy's wishes clash with Daddy's. One of two things usually happens—the sad little boy is put into therapy or put out on the street. In Bill's case, it was the latter. Daddy was a stockbroker, Mama a lawyer. When you grew up in Chicago's North Shore suburbs, you learned fast that appearances meant a lot. You ever seen the flick *Ordinary People*? Uh-huh. They weren't too far off. And no one wanted to face what Bill's appearance meant. At fifteen, Bill had the misfortune to be seen by one of his father's friends hanging out on Clark Street, outside a hustler bar known as the New Flight. Bad enough Bill, still a mere boy, was outside one of the sleaziest gay bars in town, but to be wearing a red sequined minidress, stiletto heels, seamed stockings, and a blonde bouffant wig made the situation intolerable to Bill's family, who would have given body parts to maintain their white, upper-class, all-American family image. Body parts? Honey, they gave their only begotten son. How Bill's father's friend recognized him, or what the man was even doing in that part of town, Bill never had the chance to probe.

Bill's done all right by himself, and I give him a lot of credit. What a lot of people didn't realize when they looked at a drag queen was that we're often the meanest, toughest sons of bitches to walk the streets...never mind the leather boys and all that crap. Drag queens, every one of us, are *survivors*. We've all had to make a life for ourselves against the toughest odds. Enough about that. I got the wig in place, winked at myself, and spun around.

"So give me the dirt."

Bill started to turn toward the door. If there's one thing that man hates to talk about, it's his past. I held up my hand. "Don't be goin' anywhere, child! You should know by now there's no refusing Miss Henrietta." I added, under my breath, "Except when it comes to a fuckin' raise."

Bill knew he couldn't refuse me the raise *and* a tidbit on Mr. Gary Adrion, so he came back, sat down, and started.

"My family knew the Adrions...for years...hell, maybe for generations. The country club set and all that happy horseshit. I think my grandmother used to curl with Gary's grandmother, or something."

"What do you mean, Bill? Lift weights?"

He laughed. "No, this is some game played on ice... with brooms and a big stone."

I shook my head. I had grown up in rural Alabama, and the pastimes of the rich and famous had always eluded me. Anyway.

"It's not important how we knew each other. The whole fucking group up there is inbred...the private schools, the clubs—they're all there for those people to show how much money they've got and to push those that don't out.

"Anyway, you should be nice to Gary. Not only is he one of the most beautiful boys to come out of the North Shore...he's had a hard life, that kid."

"What do you mean?"

"He's been pretty much an orphan his whole life. Raised by his grandfather, alone in some big house on Lake Michigan. In Winnetka, I think, but all those little holier-than-thou towns up there kind of blend together."

"Where were his parents?"

Bill smiled. "That's the good part. Sounds like some kind of romance story."

Ah, romance, I thought...the last refuge of the unimaginative.

"Gary's mother was a local beauty...prom queen material for sure. You know the type, that Farrah Fawcett glamour girl thing goin' on, but with this air of reserve that made her seem vulnerable and distant all at the same time. You just wanted to stare at her for hours. This combination was so potent that Diana—that was her name—was actually very unpopular with the boys, who, I think, were just intimidated by her. So Diana went off and met herself a soldier.

"This guy was not the right kind of material at all, if you catch my drift. Grew up in Waukegan, which put him squarely on the wrong side of the tracks. No plans for college. In fact, he had already been drafted for Vietnam when he met Diana. Against all the odds, they fell passionately in love. As so often happens, her family's disapproval only made things worse. She ended up going with him to San Antonio, I think, and marrying the guy so she could live in Army housing."

I could hear outside the dressing room that it was getting close to showtime. "Cut a long story short, sweetie. I gotta go on in about five."

"Right. The boy gets shipped off to rice-paddy land and is killed in action, leaving behind Diana and a little bun in the oven he knew nothing about."

"Tragic," I mumbled, straightening a spaghetti strap on my emerald dress.

"What's really tragic is Diana had some labor complications and, just like in the great romances, died shortly after giving birth."

I stood and fanned myself. "How very fucking Scarlett O'Hara!"

"Shame on you!" Bill snapped.

I rolled my eyes. "So Gary never knew either of his parents?"

"Uh-uh."

I shook my head. The adrenaline, though, was pumping. The music cues were coming up, and I could feel the preshow electricity in the air, crackling. I headed toward the door. "I can sympathize with everything, honey, but suffering."

I didn't look back to see Bill's reaction. I didn't need to.

Chapter Six

GARY

I'm waiting for Henrietta to come home from the club. It's funny, you know someone for a month, and yet there is still so little you really know. Down at the Façade—where I've been spending quite a few evenings, watching Henrietta dance, sing, and insult the audience, to their delight—everything is glitz and glamour, and I would just expect that aura of sophistication and otherworldliness to follow her home.

That's not the case. Perhaps if I had been seeing more of Liam, he would have told me what to expect. But my time has been filled with Henrietta lately, and I haven't much left over for Liam. Henrietta is a rainbow, Liam a shade of sensible gray. Can you blame me?

Henrietta's home is more what I would expect from Liam. I anticipated wild color combinations on the walls, futuristic or antique—art deco? art nouveau?—furnishings. Instead everything here is sensible, right down to the Near North location. Henrietta, like me, lives in a high-rise, fronted by floor-to-ceiling windows that look south. I can see the John Hancock, Lake Point Tower, Aon Center, all those trademarks of the Chicago skyline. Inside, the walls are parchment-colored and the furniture is warm, heavy...tans and browns in leather and suede, all what I suppose one would call contemporary.

And the biggest surprise of all, Henrietta has a husband. Again, not what I expected. I would have guessed some Italian or at least European man, with dark hair, chiseled features, and lots of muscles. But Brian is nothing like that. One look at him and you'd mumble "Accountant." Short, wispy blond hair, oval wire-rim glasses, a middle that's just a shade too thick, dressed in khakis and a denim shirt. He's made me comfortable while I wait, brewing coffee and calling my attention to the *Atlantic Monthly*s and *Scientific American*s in the magazine rack.

Brian has the air of the put-upon about him. In the way he rolls his eyes when we speak of Henrietta, the laugh that is not quite mirth-filled when I mention one of her antics on stage, I can see a man who loves another very much but perhaps knows this is his cross to bear. I immediately sense that Henrietta is not a good subject for discussion.

Brian mentions another shocker. He and Henrietta have tickets for the Chicago Symphony Orchestra that night. I laugh, and Brian cocks his head.

"What's so funny?" he asks with genuine curiosity.

I shake my head. "Just a funny thought. Sorry. What are you seeing?"

Brian closes his eyes in rapture. "They're doing a Smetana program tonight. It'll be transporting."

I nod. "I love the masters. They've survived the years."

"That's why they're called classics."

"And Henrietta? Does she share your enthusiasm?"

"Yes, I suppose," Brian says, just a touch of fatigue. "Although Henrietta has a love for dance music that I quite abhor. Industrial...relentless rhythms that sound the same over and over for twenty minutes."

I have to be fair. Much of the "dance" music played at the Façade is just like that. Even when you venture out on the dance floor, you feel as if you're standing in place after a while. I remembered a line Henrietta had once uttered and thought Brian would approve. "You know, I never talk during good music. With bad music, though, I feel it's one's duty to drown it out with conversation."

For the first time, Brian laughs. "You sound just like Henrietta."

Before we can comment further on the subject of bad music, Henrietta arrives, laden down with shopping bags, flowing into the room in rose-patterned tulle and high heels, smelling of Passion.

"Gary! What a pleasant surprise! Pick up that mug, sweetie, and come into my room. I want to show you my purchases."

I barely pick up on the sigh that escapes Brian's lips as I follow Henrietta.

*

"You're what?" Henrietta is aghast. Her laugh, tinkling, rebounds off the mustard-colored walls of her bedroom, which sports a large four-poster bed, heavy draperies, and a real oriental rug.

"You heard me. I'm in love."

"Child, you're too young to even know what love is, let alone be in it. Tell me it isn't true."

"Oh, it's true all right," I say, pausing for a moment to think of the reason for today's visit, a young girl whose beauty knows no bounds, Zoe D'Angelo. "I wasn't looking for it. In fact, I don't know what I was looking for when I found her. Excitement, maybe. And I found that...and so much more." Zoe rises up before me, the pale skin, milky white, and the pale green eyes that contrast so wonderfully with her long, thick hair that's so black it gives off a sheen of blue. And then there are her long, delicate limbs, bound up in a kind of grace that's almost feline.

Henrietta busies herself putting away her things—sequined gowns, spike-heeled shoes, silk hosiery. "Don't tell me this. You have too much to offer to let it go to waste so soon."

I laugh. "I would hardly say this is going to waste. I told you, Henrietta, I'm in love. This girl is the one I want to spend my life with. Believe it."

Henrietta slowly shakes her head as she holds up a jade minidress to her front, admiring herself in the floor-to-ceiling mahogany pedestal mirror in the corner. "Don't even be playing with me! Don't you know that men and women get together for two reasons?"

I purse my lips, waiting for another of Henrietta's pronouncements. "And what, pray tell, might those be?"

"Men out of fatigue and women out of curiosity." She puts the dress in a closet, hanging it in a row of other dazzling creations, and slams shut the closet door. She turns to me. "Both are disappointed."

"Well, there's an exception to every rule." I cross the room and look out of Henrietta's bedroom windows. With the approach of autumn, the color of the lake has changed from aqua to a more depressing gray...a harbinger of the winter to come.

"Where did you meet this little tramp?"

"Henrietta..." I warn, frowning. "I won't let you talk about Zoe that way. She is unspoiled, and not even your razor tongue can change that."

"All right, so where?"

I shrug and feel my scalp prickle. When I tell Henrietta where I met Zoe, I'm sure she'll decide the epithet "tramp" fits. I will try to explain.

"I don't know how to describe the feeling I've been having lately. Restless, I guess. When everything's been given to you all your life, everything except love, you get to a certain point where you begin to wonder if there is anything more for you. Know what I mean?"

"Sugar, I grew up poor in Alabama. Don't think you have a sympathetic ear if you want to whine about being rich." She winks. "I heard all about your trust fund. Go on."

"Well, whatever the reason, I've been bored lately. One night last week, after your show, I went down to South Halsted, down by Greektown? Definitely not the gay section of Halsted."

"Oh no, Mr. Gary wouldn't be caught dead there."

"Shut up, Henrietta, and let me finish. I know it's not the safest part of town, but I thought I'd wander a little, take in the atmosphere." I laugh. "Seedy urban decadence.

"There was a dance club just a little north of Greektown, a place called the Rock. It's one of those 'gentlemen's' clubs, a glorified strip club, really. But classy, I guess. I really hadn't been in one of these places. There was a guy outside, handing out flyers. I took one, and on the cover was a picture of her, of Zoe D'Angelo. I thought she was beautiful, so much so it almost took my breath away. If she looks this good in a photograph, well, she couldn't possibly be that good in person. I've learned about airbrushing and stuff like that from Liam. But I wanted to see for myself.

"It wasn't bad inside. I have to give them credit. It was a large loft kind of place...might have been a factory at one time. Cement floors and exposed brick walls, overhead piping painted in primary colors. White-on-white furniture and a fancy lighting system with lots of neon. I sat down and ordered a drink, just in time for the appearance of Zoe.

"I swear, Henrietta, the room disappeared when she walked out. I felt like we were all alone. Zoe was grace personified. I know that sounds corny, but if you could see her long, delicate limbs, her black hair..."

Henrietta lights a cheroot, exhales, and says, "Boy's got it bad, and that ain't good."

"Oh, but it is! You should have seen her dance! I mean, the other girls, they were nothing compared to her. They *were* strippers, but Zoe was a dancer. Her movements were like ballet, so much grace, so delicate. It was silent when she danced...no hoots, no whistles, no catcalls. And I mean it, she was the most beautiful girl there. But her movements were art, Henrietta, *art*. She doesn't belong there. And the very next night, I went backstage and told her just that.

"The funny thing was, she had noticed me too. It was as if she was waiting for me to come backstage." I lower my eyes to the floor, sheepish in the face of Henrietta's cynicism. "Since that night, I've been with her every night."

"Locked in an embrace, I'm sure."

"You don't understand."

"Honey, I'm a showgirl too. I know what goes on. How do you think I met Brian?"

"It's not like that! Sure, there's a physical part...but there's so much more. Zoe is the love of my life. I can tell you with perfect certainty I'll never want anyone else."

Henrietta rolls her eyes. "People that say things like that make me want to puke." She laughs. "It's boring, you know, loving one person all your life. It doesn't happen. People who say it does are just unimaginative and complacent. The only reason people hang on is because they're afraid someone else will pick up what they threw away."

"I feel sorry for you. You're awful, Henrietta. I don't know if I'll ever tell you anything again!" I say, but it's tempered with a smile.

"As long as you live, child, you'll tell me everything."

I shake my head.

"If those glorious hands ever commit a crime, you'll come running to your Henrietta. Right?"

I say nothing but know she is right.

"Does Liam know about this?"

I feel a hot rush of shame. "I haven't seen Liam lately. He's called a few times, left me a couple of emails, but what with spending all my free time with Zoe, I haven't gotten back to him."

"It's okay, honey. He's been busy too. Getting to be quite the success. Funny thing, his holograms lately have been moving in another direction...away from the freaks and the mondo slices of life *I* thought he was so good at...into more conventional things...more beautiful people." She snorts and looks me up and down. "Like you." Henrietta yawns. "That's the way it is in this country. Art and sex—the safer it is, the more approval you get. Anyway, I've always said that a fascinating artist does not make a fascinating person."

"I should call him."

"Yes, you should. Don't forget your old friends in favor of a little poon." She shrieks with laughter. "I mean it!" She kicks off her heels and collapses on the bed. "Miss Henrietta needs her beauty rest. You just remember. Harvesting in the spring always leads to disappointment, if you catch my drift."

"You're full of shit."

"Whatever."

I begin to head toward the door. Henrietta is reclining on the bed, never subtle. At the door, I pause, liking the drama and hoping Henrietta will appreciate it. "By the way, I've asked her to marry me."

I close the door without waiting for her reaction.

Chapter Seven

ZOE

Mother was watching me. She was *always* watching me. I appreciated the love and attention behind it, but it gave me the creeps. I mean, she thought she knew all about dancing, but things were different in her day. She wanted less. For her, it was enough to be a headliner at a strip club. Bella Donna, they called her...the Roman Goddess. The footlights, the crowds, and the fancy costumes she spent half the money she made on were enough. That was in the days before lap dances.

"Zoe."

Mother's gaze wandered over the clothes I had put out on the bed.

"Why don't you let me make you something nice, honey?"

She exhaled some smoke over the costumes lying there like dolls, waiting to be picked up and played with. She coughed, and I thought again how frequent that cough had become and how her voice had changed from throaty and sexy to raspy and dry. I wondered when she would come home from a doctor's appointment and tell me she had lung cancer.

"I can still sew, you know. Back in my day, I used to make all my costumes...made some for the other girls too.

Why, I bet you'd knock 'em dead if I did a little work on one of my old numbers."

"Mother, things aren't the same. I couldn't move in those old dresses of yours. Don't you understand? This is dance for me, not burlesque."

A look of hurt crossed her features. It had always been this way, from as far back as I can remember. She was the child and I was the parent. I rushed over to her and took one of her gnarled hands in mine. "I don't mean that what I do is any better than what you did," I said, knowing I was lying, but lying in this context couldn't be a sin. "It's just different. The clubs aren't what they used to be. And when I come out, I need to be wearing tights and light, frilly things...like this." I picked up a skirt made of swatches of ivory illusion. Thin and transparent, the skirt let me leap and spin with no impediment.

"Well, all I can say—" Mother lit another Newport off the butt of the last. "—is that people don't know a good thing when they see it. In my day, stripping was an art. It wasn't as in-your-face as what you girls do today. Lap dances." Mother blew out a stream of smoke disgustedly.

"Mother, I've never done a lap dance, and you know it."

"I also know that Ted is pressuring you to do what all the other girls do...the table dances, the lap dances. What are you going to do about *that*? You can't expect special treatment, not when Ted has been so good to us."

I crossed to the window of our third-story flat and looked out at the brick wall across the alley. I suppose Ted, in a way, had been good to us. Mother had known him for years, when he was just a maligned warm-up comedian for the showgirls. Yes, he had given us a place to live above the club, although it was nothing to boast about, a tiny one-bedroom apartment where the bathtub drain always clogged and we had to be on constant vigilance with boric acid to keep the cockroaches away. And he had let me dance there, fresh out of ballet school. It certainly wasn't my dream, but who knew how many girls competed for one spot in a company? Mother had convinced Ted, now a balding, thick-middled older man with a cigar permanently affixed to the corner of his mouth, that I was a legitimate dancer and would have to treated that way. I don't think Ted saw he had any other choice. I was good-looking—all right, some say beautiful—and knew how to move, and he needed someone. As long as I agreed to strip down to a G-string, he didn't care how many jetés or pliés I did, as long as my tits were out by the end of the number. But lately customers had been complaining, calling me snooty for turning down their money for table and lap dances.

"You're gonna have to get with the program, sugar, or I can't afford to keep you on."

His words chilled me. There was a point where I couldn't go any further, and I had already reached it. But if he let me go, Mother and I would lose the roof over our heads and the only income we had to speak of. Mother, with her emphysema, couldn't work anymore. It was almost too much just looking after me. But I couldn't do what the other girls did, couldn't hump the lap of some fifty-year-old lawyer while he stuffed money in my G-string and came in his pants. It was too much.

Thank God Prince Charming came along! I never believed I would meet someone like him in the club. I still don't understand what brought him there—it seems too lower-class for him. All the men who come in the Rock have one of two things in common; they're lonely or they're horny. The sad thing is, coming there relieves neither of those conditions. But many of them keep coming back, hoping, I guess, the next time will be different. Obviously I never wanted to play with such damaged goods. Oh sure, the occasional nice guy would come in, an out-of-towner forced to go along by his workmates or a young guy trying to be a good sport when his friends threw him a bachelor party, but for the most part they're guys who can't find their place with women in general. That's why I don't date them, even though I'm asked out on a regular basis. And with my schedule, that has pretty much meant no dates. Ironic—me, the beautiful, glamorous exotic dancer, spending her free time with her mother, watching old movies on TV and eating popcorn.

And then Prince Charming came along. I call him that because his arrival is sort of a miracle, like something out of a fairy tale. A genuinely nice guy, kind and sweet, a little shy. And of course, gorgeous! I've never seen a guy so handsome...what with his perfect lean build and a face that's, oh, how should I describe it, manly and delicate at the same time...tough yet vulnerable with these eyes that are a sort of aqua shade I've never seen before. I feel as if I've known him forever, and I started calling him Prince Charming the moment I met him. Silly. I don't even know his real name. I'm not sure I want to. Why bring down the illusion so soon?

"Do you think Prince Charming will be here tonight?" I asked Mother, who looked up from my black tights, replacing them on the bed as if they were something soiled.

Mother lit another cigarette and said, "Hmph. Prince Harming is more like it. You have to watch yourself, honey. I know what the men in these places are like."

"But he's different! That's what drew me to him in the first place."

Mother got up and crossed the room to where I stood by the window; she stroked my face, brown eyes boring into mine. "You're still so innocent." She ran her fingers through my hair. "I hope you're right. I really do. He does seem like a nice young man, a gentleman." She barked out a short laugh. "That's a bird I thought was extinct! But maybe, just maybe, he'll lead you out of here. If he could do that, he could never do wrong in my eyes."

"What are you girls babbling about? I swear to Christ, if I ever hear the words 'Prince Charming' again, I'll puke."

"Davio!" I have always loved my brother, rough-hewn yet gentle with me. He would be going away soon... He's joined the Army, and they were shipping him off to someplace in California for basic training. He leaves tomorrow. I couldn't bear the thought of it. I rushed over and hugged him, feeling the warmth of his huge, lumbering body. Davio got all the bulk while I got bird bones. We couldn't have been more different, with his sandy hair, Mother's brown eyes, and a build like a linebacker. He was no stranger to bar brawls and in one had broken his nose, which had never healed quite right. I thought it made him ruggedly handsome, but Mother was always after him to see a plastic surgeon. He never would. Davio just didn't care about things like that. "I thought you'd be gone all afternoon, getting ready for your trip."

"I'm all packed. Amazing how little I have, when it comes down to it. It all fit into two suitcases. Not that I'm going to need much, anyway, what with the Army providing everything."

He let go of me.

"I came over to see my little sister, to spend one final afternoon with her."

He gave me his lopsided grin, and I thought how much I would miss him. We had grown up together, a kind of ragtag show business family, moving all over the country. It didn't open many doors for friendships outside the family, but it made us very close.

I looked at the costume I was working on putting together and then thought *It's his last day here. I can work on that later.*

"What should we do, Davio? Did you have anything special in mind?"

"Something special is exactly what I don't have in mind. I want to have an ordinary day with you. That's what I want to remember."

"You talk like I'll never see you again!"

"Who knows? War could break out... All sorts of things could happen."

"Davio!" Mother cried. "I don't want to hear another word of it."

"So what ordinary thing?"

"It's gorgeous out there. Let's just go over to Lincoln Park and walk around, take in a little breeze off the lake. Maybe we'll find someplace good to eat lunch."

"Just let me get some jeans on."

*

Davio was right—the day was perfect. A cool breeze swept over the water, making a wonderful contrast to the hot early autumn sun, which beat down almost mercilessly. A few clouds, up high, added visual effect and little else. We walked the bike trails north of the Lincoln Park Zoo, looking, I suppose, like a young couple in love.

And that appearance was half right. I know I should have been concentrating more on my brother, but all I could think of was Prince Charming. I was eager for tonight's show to open and close so I could feel the warmth of his embrace, his smooth skin against mine. It was all I could talk about, even though I could tell Davio would have preferred to talk of almost anything else.

"Oh, Davio, don't look that way! Can't you be happy for me, just for once?" Davio had been jealous of every man who had ever paid any attention to me. He was the poster child for overly protective older brothers.

"I am happy for you, Zoe. Don't get me wrong there. It's just that I want you to be careful. In spite of what you do for a living." He sighed. "No matter what you think, *I* think you're a pretty innocent girl. You don't know how you can be taken advantage of."

"Give me a little credit. I can tell."

"Well, don't you suppose every single person who's ever been taken advantage of thought the exact same thing?"

He had a point. But all I could see were Prince Charming's blue-green eyes, his smile, the way his face lit up when he first saw me. Words can lie, but signs like those could only be the truth. I told Davio that.

"You're hopeless," he mumbled.

A gust of wind caught his fine brown hair and lifted it off his forehead. I wondered if Davio would ever meet anyone. He was pretty much a loner, always had been. But he was handsome...in a rugged sort of way. I knew women went for him. Some of the girls at the club were always asking about him, but he never pursued any of the leads I gave him. Dancers, he said, were not his type.

"He's the only guy I've ever met that I've felt this way about. Don't you see? I'm in love for the first time."

Davio scowled, the corners of his mouth turning down, a light dying in his brown eyes. "You don't even know his name."

"His name is Prince Charming." I giggled.

Davio shook his head. "You think that's funny? Why hasn't this guy ever told you his name?"

"Oh, I'm sure he would, but this has been just like a fairy tale. And that's what I think of him as...this fairy-tale prince who's come to rescue me from the evil world."

"Hopeless," Davio repeated.

"You're the one!" I skipped over to a bench. "Let's sit for a while and watch the sailboats." The lake's blue waters were dotted on the horizon with a veritable regatta, boats enjoying the last of the warm weather. Soon they would be gone, in winter storage, while the lake turned colder and gray.

We sat on the bench for a while, not saying much. Davio looked behind him, away from the lake, at the traffic whooshing by on Lake Shore Drive. He'd always been fascinated by cars...vintage, racing. The Chicago Auto Show was an annual event not to be missed, for him.

As he was looking at what I thought was the wrong view, I saw him. Prince Charming. He was a little north of us, pedaling a mountain bike, his short hair blown back away from his face. For some reason I wanted to enjoy him like this, when he was completely unaware of my presence. Just to drink in his beauty, like some wild animal caught in the woods, untouched by my gaze. I whispered to Davio. "There he is."

Davio turned and looked south, toward the city. By the time I had directed him the right way, Prince Charming was nothing more than a dot among the other cyclists and rollerblades, a broad expanse of navy cotton T-shirt across his back.

Davio squinted.

"He's too far, but that's him."

I was surprised by the anger that creased his features.

"So that's our Prince Charming."

"Davio, stop."

"I swear, Zoe, if he ever lays one hand on you, if he ever does even the tiniest thing to hurt you... I'll kill him."

I laughed, but his words chilled me. He was serious.

Chapter Eight

DAVIO

The hours were passing more quickly, winding down toward the inevitable—the plane I would board tomorrow, leaving Zoe and everything else behind. It was for the best, I supposed. I needed some sort of purpose in my life, some order, and I suspected the Army would provide it.

Zoe and I had eaten lunch on the lakefront, buying hot dogs and chips from a little cart. I wished I could always have her like this...to myself. I almost always had, but now Prince Charming had come along and spoiled everything.

When we got home, Zoe went into the bedroom for a nap. She had become a real night owl, although I suspected this wasn't her true nature. But her show wasn't over until nearly 2:00 a.m., and what with this Prince Charming character coming around, I expect she didn't get to sleep until the sky was lightening over the lake. Bad for a young girl. She needed her rest.

Alone with Mother, we made chitchat about what the Army held in store for me, what time my plane would leave tomorrow, what I expected out of the Army.

Something had been bothering me for a long time, years, I suppose. And now, on the eve of my leaving, I thought I should get up the nerve to ask Mother about it. I know there wasn't a war on or anything, but who knew, when a guy went away to the Army, if he would come back. I didn't want to die not knowing the truth. I knew it would embarrass her, knew it and didn't give a good fuck. I had a right to know.

"Mother, there's something I've always wanted to know."

I saw immediately the look that crossed her features, as if something inside was closing up. She still retained the brassy blonde hair, the rouge on the sagging cheeks, and the bosom that had once made her a living, but a certain shine left her dark eyes, and her smile vanished the moment I spoke.

"What, Davio?" she said with no enthusiasm.

"Well, you only have to look at Zoe and me." I stopped. I didn't know how to put this. "We're different as night and day. Don't look a thing alike. No one has ever guessed I'm her brother."

"You're her brother!" Mother snapped.

I put up a hand to silence her, to defend myself against the accusations I was sure were already forming in her mind. We had gotten close to this subject many times in the past, but I had never had the guts to bring it up directly before. "Zoe and me, we don't have the same dad, do we?"

With a trembling hand, Mother lit another cigarette. She drew the smoke in deeply, looking everywhere in the room but at me, and exhaled.

"What the fuck? Why not? No, Davio, your father is someone else. There, are you satisfied?"

"I just think I have a right to know, is all." I didn't want to whine. "Who was he?"

"Don't you worry, Davio, you come from the finest stock. Your father was a gentleman. He was loaded, and he was...married. I always thought he'd leave his wife and kids for me, thought it for years. That's what the 'other woman' always thinks. Married guys have relied on it for years." She leaned closer to me at the little kitchen table. "And we were always careful. But accidents happen." She bit her lower lip. "When I got pregnant, I thought maybe it would be enough to get him away from his family, but that right there pretty much put an end to things."

"The fucker."

"No, Davio, it wasn't like that! He was a good man. He gave me a lot of money, but he had his obligations, honey. He couldn't leave them behind."

"Uh-huh. So Zoe and me are only half siblings?"

Mother nodded. "He was a gentleman, really, not like the types that usually hung around."

"You sound like Zoe, talking about her Prince Charming," I sneered.

"This Prince Charming fellow may turn out to be a very good thing for Zoe. He just might be her ticket out of here."

Already the wheels were turning in Mother's head. A rich guy, setting Zoe up for life. Dance lessons, European vacations, the best of everything. And of course, living quarters for Mother, which she could decorate with old flyers from her shows and the publicity photos she kept carefully guarded in a leather-bound album.

"You mean like you thought my father was?"

She didn't have anything to say to that, just stared at her lap. I waited for her to say something else, and when she didn't, I stood up.

"I'm gonna go have one more peek at Zoe before I go. That all right?"

She lit a cigarette off the butt of the last and stared at the floor. "Just look," she mumbled.

*

The air in Zoe's tiny bedroom was close, being moved around pretty inefficiently by a box fan in the window. The bathroom off the bedroom was a riot of cosmetics, conditioners, and moisturizers, covering about every available surface.

Women.

I did them a favor and shook the Drano into the tub and sink's drains. The damn things were always clogging on them, and they didn't keep after them as well as they should.

I went back into the bedroom and watched my sister, wearing an old oversized T-shirt and a pair of shorts, curled on one side, sleeping. Her black eyelashes seemed so long, and the innocence as she lay there asleep almost—what?—radiated off her.

I wanted so much to lean down and kiss her. I had to settle for just leaning close, to feel her warm breath on my face. I brushed a strand of sweaty hair from her forehead. It was all I could do not to touch her. It's always been all I could do. I wanted Zoe. In more rational moments I could deny my feelings, call them brotherly love, but there was something dark under that. I wanted to fuck her.

There, I said it. It was only me listening anyway. And the tightness in my jeans wouldn't be pacified with a lie. I suppose it helped a little that Zoe and I were only half siblings. Cheap rationalization, but there you go.

I imagined lying with her and taking her in my arms, looking into her eyes when she awakened, all surprised. I would kiss her then, do all the things that only once in a great while I permitted myself to fantasize about.

Stop. I knelt beside her, laying my hand close to hers. "I meant what I said back there, little sister. I'll kill anyone who ever harms you...even in the least."

I got up and hurried from the room. Enough was enough.

Chapter Nine

LIAM

"You've got to be joking!" I gasped when Henrietta told me the news. "Gary Adrion's getting married? Where did you hear such rot?"

"Right from the horse's mouth, honey. By the way, speaking of horses, that hologram had a little too many dramatic shadows, if you know what I mean. A girl could go blind squinting. How is our Mr. Adrion hung, anyway?"

"Oh, stop it! Now what do you mean, he told you he wants to get married?"

"I mean he wants to get a license, slip a ring on that girl's finger, and say that old until death do us part lie." Henrietta laughed.

I shook my head. "You are absolutely incorrigible. Is nothing sacred to you?"

"Good looks...and money."

Henrietta kept an absolutely straight face when she said this. I didn't dare challenge her. I hadn't seen her in a while, and it was good to be in her company again. I could always go anywhere with her and not get that much attention because she bears no resemblance whatsoever to a man. With her delicate limbs and fine-boned facial structure, most men would laugh at you if you even attempted to tell the truth. Henrietta had called earlier that afternoon, with her usual blustery I-won't-take-no-for-an-answer bravado, gossipy and telling me she had something important to tell me. I suggested we meet up at the Nervous Center, a little cafe on Lincoln Avenue that made the best Thai iced coffee in town. Besides, I loved its funky atmosphere...the thrift store furniture, the lamps crafted from old vacuum cleaners, the eclectic reading material on the shelves, and the music, which was a bizarre mix of things like cha-cha and atonal minimalist compositions. I couldn't believe the painfully young man I had just met a couple of months ago was already planning to marry someone. The idea was preposterous, and I said so.

"Who gets married in this day and age at twenty-one?"

"Obviously, our boy Gary." Henrietta took a sip of her cappuccino.

I shook my head again. It seemed it had been all I did since hearing the news. A young man with beauty like that... There was so much ahead of him. Why tie himself down with one person practically before he had even stopped growing? I had hoped he would model for me some more...for my commercial photography. I was always getting jobs from high-paying clients like Ameritech and Motorola, and I'm sure I could have given him a steady stream of work, but he wasn't all that interested. "It seems like such a waste."

"The one big disadvantage to getting married," Henrietta said, and I immediately thought of her husband, Brian, "is that it makes you unselfish. And unselfish people are always *boring*."

"I know you don't mean that."

"Right. You just keep on thinking so highly of me, dear."

"Well, we should be heading out. We don't want to be late for our reservations."

We were meeting Gary for dinner at Madame Ing's, a French-Vietnamese restaurant in Boystown on Halsted Street. I thought it would be fun to show him off. And I'd be lying if I didn't admit I wanted, just a little, to be seen in his company. "Maybe we can talk some sense into him."

"Don't count on it." Henrietta ground her cheroot into an ashtray and stood to follow me out.

*

As I watched Gary walk into the restaurant, I knew there would be no chance of talking him out of anything. Even before he saw us, he was beaming. There was an imperceptible glow about him that positively radiated. The jauntiness in his step made him seem as if he were walking a few inches above the floor. I felt myself go weak at the splendor of him.

"Gary!" I stood. I knew I was beaming too. He had that effect on me. I can't deny it.

He smiled, and I swear every conversation in the room paused, heads turning to look. He hurried to our table, a little breathless. "I suppose Ma Bell here has already told you my good news."

"Watch it, honey. You don't want to start name-calling with me. I'll put you in your place so fast you won't know what hit until tomorrow...or the next day."

"I believe it."

Gary sat at the table with us. He was full of energy. He reminded me of a little boy with a new toy on Christmas. He grabbed my hand, and even though he was unaware, the touch sent a jolt of electric longing through me. I withdrew my hand, but he continued.

"I've met the most wonderful girl, Liam."

"So I heard."

The waiter arrived to take our orders, and I was almost grateful for the delay. For some reason I didn't want to see this happen, and not talking about it was a way, ineffectual at best, of keeping reality at bay.

"Zoe D'Angelo. Zoe D'Angelo. Zoe D'Angelo. It's unusual, isn't it? But she's the most beautiful woman in the world, Liam. Once you see her, you'll want to photograph her. She has the most glorious pale-green eyes, black hair, fine-boned."

He closed his eyes, and I watched rapture transform his features. It was hard for me to say anything against the union, but still it seemed stupid to marry so young.

"Are you sure, Gary? I mean, you did just turn twenty-one. There's still so much in store for you."

"Isn't it better to enjoy all that's in store with someone I love passionately by my side?"

It was hard to argue with his enthusiasm. "But it's so sudden, so quick..." I said weakly.

"Don't try to spoil this for me." Gary leaned closer to Henrietta and me. "I want you guys to come see her dance tonight. Don't say no. I already had Zoe reserve a table right at the front for us."

"Where did you say she performed?"

"The Rock," Henrietta blurted, cutting into a spring roll, a smirk affixed to her face.

"The Rock? But that's a strip club, isn't it?"

Gary rolled his eyes. "Exotic dancers," he corrected.

"Uh-huh. Big difference." The smirk didn't leave Henrietta's face for a second.

Gary shook his head. "Don't pay any attention to that jaded old queen."

Henrietta sat up straighter in her seat. "You better watch your mouth, boy. This is my last warning, I swear."

Gary laughed in response to her. "Zoe's had all kind of ballet training, and it shows. She elevates the whole place to another realm when she's on stage. You'll see."

*

When we had finished dinner, Gary took my hand again. "Listen, Henrietta's giving me a ride." Henrietta owned a Mazda Miata...a two-seater. "Would you be horribly offended if I asked you to take a cab?" He looked so concerned, so apologetic, that I couldn't help but burst into laughter.

I held up a hand. "It's no problem. I'll see you there."

I watched as the two left the restaurant, draining my coffee cup. I had a weird feeling, not quite sadness, but a feeling as if I had suddenly grown years older.

I chalked it up to my misgivings about Gary's rash decision. But I knew there was something more to it.

Chapter Ten

GARY

Seen through Liam and Henrietta's eyes, the Rock is a different sort of club. I've noticed this phenomenon before, how you can gain a whole new perspective when you see something as you think others might see it for the first time. Usually it's a good thing, but this time I see the Rock as a little more tawdry, a little more run-down than I had ever noticed. The walls need a new coat of paint. The floor is dirtier than I remember, littered with cigarette butts and grit. The tables seem cheap, as if they were bought by the gross from Kmart, cheap laminate and aluminum legs. But I know these things will just contrast all the more with Zoe's artistry, making her shine all the brighter against these dull surroundings.

"Oh!" Henrietta exclaims, "I just love places like this. The province of the horny and downtrodden. Who says this kind of place can't be some sort of wholesome entertainment for the masses?"

Liam shakes his head and sits gingerly at one of the tables. "So this is where your true love plies her trade."

I sit too and call over one of the girls, ordering bourbon and water for Liam, a martini for Henrietta, and a cider for myself. "Don't be sarcastic, Liam," I warn. "It doesn't suit you."

The place is filled to capacity tonight. The heavy bass of the dance music makes it difficult for us to talk, yet the roar of conversation and throaty male laughter rebounds off the walls. There is an expectancy in the air, an electric tingling that runs through the music and the laughter, and I know it's all for Zoe. I've seen it happen again and again, how quiet the room becomes when she comes out to dance, how the crowd is mesmerized by her. I feel almost a tingling, knowing this woman belongs to me. That this artist with movement and form loves only me.

I grab Liam's hand, and he looks at me with surprise. "Just a few minutes more and you'll understand completely why I love her."

Liam sips his drink and doesn't move his hand. In fact, his finger gently strokes the side of my hand. I smile at him, pat his hand, and lift mine away.

"She's been trained in ballet, you know. And it shows."

Finally the house lights dim and the last dance tune ends. The people on the dance floor make their way to their seats as a single spotlight shines down on the stage. Warmth fills me. I am so proud of her! I can't wait for Liam and Henrietta to see.

"Ladies and gentlemen," a voice booms from offstage. "Please welcome Ms. Zoe D'Angelo!"

The crowd erupts with cheers, and I sit back, almost gloating. Once the applause dies down, the music begins, Peggy Lee singing "Fever." The stage goes black for an instant as the clapping and cheering dies down to silence. Then the spot comes back up and there she is, almost glowing in a black bodysuit with a tattered skirt of white nylon illusion. Her long black hair is loose, and her tiny feet are encased in a pair of ballet slippers.

Liam leans over to me and whispers, "She's beautiful, Gary. I can't argue with your taste. Simply stunning. Bring her around. We'll do a session."

I beam. "Oh, I will. I will. Once we're married, I want to take her away from here. She needs to do something legitimate...a real dance company. Your photographs could be her calling card."

"Of course," Liam whispers and sits back, watching.

I look to Henrietta, who sips her martini, her golden-eyed gaze never leaving the stage. She doesn't have to say anything. If anyone appreciates beauty in the female form, it's a drag queen. Hell, they've made their whole lives a kind of homage to feminine beauty.

And Zoe begins to move. She starts with a graceful leap, only it's not so graceful. She comes down with an audible thud on the stage. Although she didn't quite stumble, her landing was awkward and heavy.

"Ouch."

Henrietta giggles, and I assure her that it was only a momentary lapse. Henrietta pats my hand.

"Don't worry about it, honey. She's probably a little nervous. She knows you brought your friends tonight, doesn't she?"

I nod and continue to watch. The movements, though, do not improve. Her twirls are leaden, and I almost expect her to stumble dizzily when she ends what was once a graceful pirouette across the stage. There are a few titters from the audience.

The tempo and the beat of the music speed up, and Zoe doesn't seem aware of the shift. She continues to plod through her routine, one I've seen several times before. One in which she is always so graceful that she silences the house. But now it seems as if she is two or three beats behind the music. Her movements are stiff and yes, graceless. She dances no better than any of the other girls.

She has trouble with the catch on her skirt and has to stop for a moment to undo it. She lets the flimsy material fall to the floor. There are catcalls. I have never heard anyone make any noise when Zoe dances. She used to slither out of her tights at this point, but now she resembles nothing more than a middle-aged woman struggling to get out of her pantyhose. There is more laughter from the audience.

But it's as if Zoe is unaware of their mirth. Her face is stony and expressionless, where once there was a radiant smile, the look of a confident dancer.

And then I see something I have never seen before. As Zoe lumbers across the stage in her G-string, a fat middle-aged man in a houndstooth-checked sports coat stands, a dollar held aloft in his stubby fingers.

She has become nothing more than one of the dancers, a stripper. She struggles out of her top, getting it caught on her chin, and there are wolf whistles as her breasts, in a tiny black lace brassiere, are exposed. I hang my head as men line up to tip her.

Liam and Henrietta are looking at me. I can't bear the sympathy and what almost looks like pity on their faces. "Just go," I hiss.

Liam nods, and I can see his relief. As they are getting up, Henrietta places a hand on my shoulder, leans over, and whispers, "It's all right, honey. She is beautiful. What I wouldn't give to look like that girl."

I close my eyes, shutting her out. I keep my eyes closed until the music ends, until the laughter and applause dies down.

My Zoe, my Zoe, where have you gone to?

*

After the show, I get up, nausea roiling in my stomach. I feel an anger so strong it makes my hands tremble. How could this have happened? How could she have been some new-age Isadora Duncan one night and an awkward Blaze Starr the next?

"Hey, bud, how's it goin'?" Ted greets me. I don't reply as I storm through the cloud of cigar smoke surrounding him.

Zoe sits, far too calmly, I think, at her dressing room table. Her face is smeared with Vaseline, and she tissues off the pancake makeup, eyes reflected in the mirror in front of her.

When she catches sight of me in the mirror, she smiles and hurries to finish wiping off the makeup. She gets up from her seat and rushes over to throw her arms around me. I stiffen within her embrace. I refuse to return it.

She leans back, a half smile on her face, searching out my gaze, which I will not return.

"What's the matter?" She giggles. "Something wrong?"

"How can you ask me that?"

"What do you mean?" The smile, by degrees, vanishes.

"What do I mean? What do I mean! How do you explain that outrage on the stage tonight? Zoe, what got into you?"

The smile comes back again, but it doesn't warm me anymore. In fact, it only makes me angrier. How can she pretend not to know what's wrong?

"Oh, my Prince Charming. Don't you see? It doesn't matter anymore."

"What the fuck are you talking about?" I recoil, stepping back. I do not want her touching me. Not now, not ever again. Her dance, her movements were part of what I loved about her. How can I continue to love her when that's gone?

She tries to put her arms around me and relents when I take another step back. She cocks her head. "I love you," she whispers simply. "Nothing else matters."

"You danced horribly out there!" I say, my voice trembling. I suddenly feel as if I'm about to cry. "You were no better than any of the other whores that parade around out there!"

Zoe looks as if I've slapped her. "Our love," she says. "That's all the matters."

I can see moistness brimming at the corners of her pale-green eyes.

"Once I realized how much I loved you, I knew all of this wasn't important. Don't you see? I just don't care anymore. You and me...that's all that counts. Now, don't be angry with me..."

"You embarrassed me in front of my friends." The volume is gone from my voice, but there is a low intensity to it that I think makes it even more venomous. "I was so proud of you. I talked you up to them." I turn, unable to stand the sight of her. "I've never been more humiliated."

I feel her hand on my back, tentative. "Darling, please, come upstairs with me." Her voice becomes low, seductive. "I'll make everything right again. You know I can."

I whirl on her and clench my fists to stop myself from slapping her. "You're no different from the rest. A cheap whore is all *you* are! What was I thinking? My God!"

Zoe bites her lip, struggling to hold back her tears. "What about our love? What about getting married?"

I say nothing, leaving her to squirm in my icy silence. "Fuck that," I whisper. "You've killed my love."

There's nothing more to say, and I hurry from the dressing room, Zoe's tear-filled cries behind me.

"Come back! Please! Come back!"

Chapter Eleven

ZOE

I sat alone. It didn't matter that there were two or three dancers in the dressing room with me. I sat alone.

I glanced in the mirror and saw my eyes, reddened from crying, my moist nose and trembling lip. There was no expression. The words "You've killed my love" were like some song I couldn't get out of my head, playing on endless loop. In spite of the pain they caused, they wouldn't go away, a wound I could not stop myself from worrying.

The other girls ignored me. I didn't blame them. When one of them did venture to speak to me, my stony stare, that of a dead woman, was all they got in return. I saw it in their eyes, the way they lowered their voices to whispers.

I tied my hair in a ponytail, stuffed my dance clothes in my bag, and left. Fortunately for once, I thought, I was glad I didn't live far, just above the club. Mother would be out tonight, a rare date, and I wouldn't have to endure her questions, her sympathy. I could not bear that.

I trudged up the stairs behind the stage. They were dirty, surrounded by a metal rail on one side and a crumbling brick wall on the other. They looked about as desolate as I felt.

How can he not want to be with me anymore? How can one minute life be full of promise and hope and the next offer nothing?

I put my key in the lock and opened the door, flicked on the overhead light. I went through the motions like a robot, having no feelings. I couldn't help recalling other recent nights, when Prince Charming and I would creep into the apartment, whispering and laughing, trying not to wake Mother, to hurry into my bedroom. I was no virgin—Lord, no—but with him, it really was like the first time. I hadn't known sex could be so wonderful, so fulfilling. I could see him still above me, that perfect brow knitted together with pleasure, the full lips slightly parted as his breath came faster and faster. I could still feel him inside me.

How can he be gone?

And all at once it came down on me, the despair. I shut off the light, and the apartment went silver from the glow of the full moon outside. I stumbled, knocking things over. A vase atop a bookcase shattered to the floor, and I kicked at its shards, screaming. Fortunately the thunder of the music downstairs drowned out my cries.

I wandered into the bathroom and saw the blue-and-white can of Drano Davio left on the back of the toilet earlier today. Could it have been today? That happy girl, so full of love and optimism, seemed like someone I knew a long time ago, if I ever really knew her at all.

I picked up the can of Drano and stared at it, its cold metal matching what I felt. A lump in my throat and my eyes burning, I hurried into the kitchen, grabbed a tumbler and a bottle of vodka, and returned to the bathroom.

There was no hope. No reason to go on. Without my Prince Charming, what did I have to look forward to? I popped open the cap on the Drano, twisted the lid off the vodka.

Chapter Twelve

DAVIO

Early morning has always been my favorite time of day, the city still quiet, the light in the sky a sort of grayish-blue. Even the birds hadn't yet awakened. I hurried through streets thick with early morning fog, sunlight slanting through it, just west and south of the Loop.

I needed to see Zoe one more time before I boarded that 747 for California. What with her hooking up with this so-called Prince Charming character and me being gone for who knew how long, it might be a long time before I saw her again. And when I did, we'd both be different people.

I didn't care if she was still sleeping. Just one more glance to hold in my memory before I started off on my new life. I wasn't sure how I would manage without being able to see Zoe, to hear her laughter, to pretend to be annoyed at her teasing. I hated the thought of her with another man, doing all the things I wanted to be doing with her. Wanting, really, to be that other man. Maybe in another time, Zoe and I could have been together forever.

I made a turn that would take me down the alley behind the club. It was a shortcut, and I needed one this early morning. My flight was due to take off soon, and I didn't have much time.

The first thing I noticed was a heap in the alley, formless. At least that's what I think I remember. Things became jumbled in that instant, that heart-pounding wild instant when everything changed. Panic, horror, whatever the hell you want to call it has a way of doing that to you. Let's go with the presumption that what I first saw was a heap. Let's say that I clucked my tongue at the carelessness of someone who would leave a bag of garbage in an alley when there was a dumpster not three feet away.

Even pretending, though, I knew that what lay before me, the dark shape shrouded in the mist, was not a bag of garbage. But as with so many horrible things that worm their way into our lives, our rational mind reaches for some other explanation before accepting the truth that's staring us in the face.

As I drew closer, part of me wanted to turn and run. If I backed away from what was in front of me, hurried off to catch my plane, maybe it wouldn't be real. But I'm not delusional enough for that.

I had to see.

I slowed my pace, nausea beginning to churn in my stomach, dread making me feel already as if I could puke.

The mist cleared as I neared her, as if some skeletal hand was pulling back a curtain to put on display the most horrible thing I had ever seen, gibbering at my fear. There came a point, then, when not even the fog could hide what was in front of me. I remember my throat becoming suddenly dry, as if something large and round had lodged there. My heart sped up, pounding against my chest almost painfully. A line of sweat formed at my hairline.

I closed my eyes as I stood next to her. I think a sort of low moan escaped my lips, an animal lowing in pain. I think. I can't remember for sure.

It was Zoe. Her head was twisted at an impossible angle, and a thin line of blood streamed from her ear. I knelt beside her, feeling numb, and turned her over.

She was no longer beautiful. Her face was the color of ashes, and around her mouth and nose, vivid red burns bloomed, erasing whatever life, whatever beauty had been there. What in hell had happened to her? There was a chemical stench coming from her. A thick foam had formed around her lips, which looked almost eaten away.

I gathered her up in my arms, and finally, finally—and this I know for sure—I began to scream. But my screams went unheard, either because no one was listening or no one wanted to.

Chapter Thirteen

GARY

I awaken and stumble from bed. My head pounds from the night before. My throat and nasal passages burn. When I blow my nose, the tissue is covered with blood. I stand above the toilet, letting the piss flow, one hand bracing myself against the cool tile wall, eyes shut. My stomach churns.

In bits and pieces, as I stumble back toward my bed, the night before returns. Dumping Zoe. Her tears, the tiny, sob-choked voice calling out for me to come back. I had fled that voice and eventually needed to flee from myself.

I wandered the streets. My hands were shaking. I stopped at a bar a few blocks south of the Rock. I don't remember the name. It was a dark place, no efforts toward decoration, smelling of stale beer and years of cigarette smoke. I went to the machine in the corner and bought myself a pack of Marlboros, even though I gave up the habit when I met Zoe. I guess I figured it didn't matter now. I sat at the bar, trying to think of anything but Zoe and unable to think of anything but. Straining toward oblivion, I ordered beer after beer after beer, mixing these with shots of Jack Daniel's. I wanted to get so drunk I thought of nothing. I wanted to make my head fuzzy and unable to process.

As I sat hunched over the bar, lost in a haze of gray smoke, a woman approached me.

I pass one of my windows. Fog presses in so close they appear white, opaque. I get back in bed, flinging myself on it, not bothering with blanket or sheet. Try to go back to sleep, but the face of the woman from last night swims before me.

Lesley? Was that her name? No, no, it was Lizzie. I had made lame jokes about Lizzie Borden. Forty whacks.

"You look like you just lost your best friend," she said, voice raspy from too many cigarettes. She was coarse, the exact opposite of Zoe's delicate beauty. Bleached blonde hair in a stiff, dry mane around her face, a face tanned so deeply it looked damaged, luridly made-up, red lipstick, blue eye shadow, crooked teeth that pointed inward. A donkey's laugh. She was a horror.

I don't remember what we talked about, don't remember even if we talked much after our introductions. We went to her place, a South Side studio apartment, walls grimy, black vinyl furniture, a furry white rug that I fucked her on. She wanted it up the ass, and I gave it to her savagely, right from the start, ignoring her cries of pain, her fist beating on my chest and telling me to go slower. It was all right; she settled into it. After the fucking, cocaine, which I had never done. It kept me up until fingers of blue-gray light crept in between the slats of her miniblinds.

I turn in my bed, eyes burning, everything aching, and remember getting home but not how I got here.

I sit upright in my bed suddenly, the motion causing a bright stab of pain behind my right eye.

I don't know why I want to see the hologram. Perhaps to assure myself that I'm still an innocent young man and that my innocence will show in the portrait.

I stumble, naked, into the living room, where I had set the hologram up on a marble pedestal I bought just for the purpose. I click it on...wishing I had just a couple more bumps to make things right again. I stare and stare, thinking my alcohol- and cocaine-addled brain is playing tricks with my vision. But I can't change the fact that the hologram looks as if it has been altered.

It's a simple change, really. Simple enough to cause me to wonder if the change hasn't been there all along, and I just hadn't noticed it. But I know, deep down, I'm deluding myself. The thing is different.

The mouth is really all that has changed. It looks crueler somehow, the lips taut, thinner. Yes, I finally have to admit before heading off to my bedroom, where I wonder if I will ever sleep again, the mouth looks cruel.

I turn, putting my thumb in my mouth, and throwing my other arm over my throbbing forehead, I finally sleep.

*

The next thing I know, it's afternoon. The sunlight behind my curtains and blinds peeks through the cracks, brilliant, unnerving. The phone is chirping. I roll over and pick up the cordless handset on the nightstand beside me. "'Lo," I say in a voice thick with sleep.

"You have a visitor, sir." The doorman's voice comes through the phone, inappropriately brisk. "A Miss Henrietta Wotton."

I roll my eyes. "Tell her I'm not here. Tell her you just got my answering machine. In fact, Frank, tell anyone who comes to call that I'm not in...until you hear different from me."

He says nothing, and I listen to the click of the receiver being replaced.

There is no more sleep. The headache has abated a little, and with a fatigue more pronounced than I've ever known, I place my feet on the floor and rub my eyes.

In the kitchen, I make myself a pot of coffee and sit with a mug of the steaming black stuff at the little porcelain table, fishing another Marlboro out of the pack. I sit and smoke, sipping coffee, again trying to think of nothing. But the hologram comes back. I get up wearily and go to look at it. After all, I was pretty fucked up last night. *You did not, Gary, consume any hallucinogens.*

But now, in a slightly more sober state, in spite of the clogged nose, I see even more clearly that the portrait *has* changed. There are lines around the mouth. Lines of cruelty. One might look at the portrait now and say "That is not a nice man. That's a man who doesn't have a heart." I turn away from it, feeling the queasiness rise up in my gut. I can't abide any more of this coffee, and I return to the kitchen, where I watch it flow down the drain, reddish-brown against stark white porcelain.

I can't explain how something inanimate, a recording, really, might change, but I can understand what the change means. Last night I hurt another person purposefully. All of this short life, I've tried never to do that. My grandfather, who raised me, was a cold son of a bitch, never giving me any real attention or love. Hell, Christmases often passed like any other day.

I never wanted to be anything like him.

I realize that if cruelty could change the portrait, perhaps kindness could change it back. I sit and think of Zoe, then pull some stationery out of the desk drawer.

I write to Zoe, trying to find words that can express how deeply sorry I am. They are elusive, straining to escape my pinning them down on the page. But I finally am able to compose something that is suitably apologetic, that decries my cruelty of the night before and declares that I really do love her. I tell her I was off balance the night before. I didn't mean what I said. And last, of course, I want to marry her.

Just as I put the letter in an envelope, the phone rings again.

"The same woman is here again, sir. She won't accept that you aren't up there. What should I do?"

I sigh. "Send her up."

When I open the door to admit her, Henrietta does not seem her usual self, sassy and sarcastic. No gap-toothed smile graces her manila-porcelain skin.

"What happened to you?" She walks into the apartment, cheroot smoke and my own acquiescence moving to let her pass.

I rub my head and grin. "Bad night last night."

She takes my hand. "I know, honey. And Miss Henrietta's here to comfort you."

"I already tried that. It didn't work. Time's the only thing that's going to make things better."

"Truer words..." she says, crossing the living room to pull up the blinds, flooding the room with sunlight and a sky so blue it could only belong to early autumn.

"Oh, man." I slump down into a leather chair, feeling its smooth coolness on the back of my neck. "I wish I could just go back and do that whole fucking night over."

"It was horrible," Henrietta says. "But you'll get over it."

I bark out a short, mirthless laugh. "What do you know about it?" It almost seems as if Henrietta knows how I spent my night after she and Liam left me at the Rock.

Henrietta cocks her head. "Didn't you read my email?" She gets up and moves so she stands above me, eyes meeting mine. "Haven't you read the paper today?"

"What are you talking about?" Her gaze, full of some weird sort of sympathy, unnerves me. Something cold scuttles down my spine. I wish I hadn't let her in. Something bad is coming; I can feel it waiting in the wings...something dark.

Henrietta grabs my chin and forces me to look at her. "You don't know, do you?"

I don't know what she's talking about. I turn my head roughly to release myself from her grasp.

I get up to follow her as she moves into the kitchen.

"Honey, sit down." She pulls out a chair for me. She fills the mug I left on the counter with coffee and places it before me. "I'll ask again. Did you read my email?"

"No, no. I haven't even turned the fucking computer on. What's going on?"

Henrietta closes her eyes for a moment, as if an unbearable pain is passing behind her eyelids. When she opens them, she bites her lip.

"I can't stand the suspense, Henrietta."

"She's dead. Oh, Gary, I am so sorry. I thought you knew. I thought that's why you looked so horrible." A trembling hand flutters up to her mouth, covering it. She removes it and says, "Zoe D'Angelo killed herself last night. It was in the *Tribune* this morning. Her brother found her body in an alley behind the club." Henrietta hung her head and whispered, "She drank Drano and vodka and flung herself out of her apartment window."

I feel almost as if a current of electricity has passed through me, leaving me weak and gasping. I run to the sink and vomit, yellow bile splashing against cold porcelain.

"It can't be true!" I scream when I've composed myself enough to speak. I think of the letter I just wrote her, a proclamation of love and sorrow, reiterating my desire that we spend our lives together. She will never see it now. The loss makes me sick, so sick I'm not sure I can stand. I grope my way across the kitchen and collapse heavily into a chair. "Go in there," I say, pointing to the dining room where my desk is. I hardly have the strength to put much breath behind my words. "Get the letter that's lying on top and bring it here." This is completely unreal. I feel a strange numbness that makes my head feel heavy, as if it has doubled in size. I want to curl into a ball, sleep, never waken.

Henrietta comes back, the sage-colored envelope in her hand. She looks at me, brows furrowed, questioning.

"Just read the damn thing," I whisper. I want someone to know I'm not the heartless bastard Zoe must have thought me before she killed herself.

Henrietta sits to read the letter. It takes only a moment. She puts it down. "Now, honey, you listen to me. I know you're feeling horrible, feeling *responsible* just now—anyone would—but this is not your fault. It's never anyone's fault when someone decides to off themselves. There are always alternatives...for all of us. Lord knows I've had my heart broken enough to want to kill myself, but there was always something out there. Suicide's for the weak."

"Don't say that. Don't you say anything bad about her."

Henrietta holds up a finger. "A long time ago I decided *no one* was going to tell me not to say *anything*. Just listen to me. Suicide is selfish. That's it, plain and simple." Henrietta shook her head. "She was a beautiful girl, and I'm sure kind and sweet and good to her mother, but what she did last night was a selfish act. You dumped her after the show, didn't you?"

I nodded.

"All of us, sooner or later, get dumped." A smile flashes across her features. "Maybe it won't happen to you, though. Anyway, she was only thinking of herself last night. She wasn't thinking of whatever kind of family she has or anyone who loves her. It was a cruel, heartless thing to do to them." Henrietta sits back and lights up. Smoke billows around her face.

I think of Zoe's mother, a coarse woman who couldn't be more different from her daughter. There's nothing subtle about Mrs. D'Angelo. But she worshipped Zoe. I could see that the moment Zoe and I met...the protective way she had with her daughter. The look in her eyes as she touched her, helping her backstage. I know this woman will be out of her mind with grief this morning. And then there's a brother; what's his name? Davio. I hadn't yet had the chance to meet him, but from Zoe's description, he all but put her on a pedestal and bowed down before it. He had been the one who found her body. I begin to see Henrietta's logic. I think of Davio D'Angelo this morning, how his life must feel perhaps even more ruined than mine. If Zoe had only had a little hope, everything would have been right...today. All she had to do was sleep on it. By the time she woke up, the letter might have already been on its way. Instead she ruined the lives of everyone who cared about her.

"And besides," Henrietta continues, "I know you don't believe this now, but you would have been miserable. I've been around a lot longer than you, sweetie, to know that this union would have made you happy for about six months, and then you'd be wretched, just wretched."

I start to challenge that, but Henrietta holds up a hand, knowing what I am about to say and stopping me.

"You listen to me. I know."

I can say nothing. But the tears are beginning to abate. It is not, after all, the end of the world.

"What you've taken part in is a tragedy. Appreciate it. It's like Shakespeare...a great romantic tragedy. Zoe's grand gesture simply makes it all the more delicious." Henrietta laughs, and for a moment, I'm horrified. Then I manage to laugh with her.

Life will go on.

"I think I want to be alone now. I'm going to light a few candles to her memory and just think of her." I smile. "Then I'll be all right."

"When you're thinking about her, think this. Women love cruelty. We thrive on it. You don't have to look too far to see that." Henrietta inhales deeply on her cheroot. "We thrive on it, honey. Besides, Zoe will live on, in a way, in the dance, in her art."

I nod. I've heard enough. Henrietta has actually done a lot of good. I wonder, though, if there is something wrong with me. Shouldn't I feel more? Where is my heart? How can I so easily be talked out of my despair?

Henrietta stands. "I'll leave you alone now."

She comes close and takes my chin in her hand, forcing me to look at her.

"Don't let this get you down. You're beautiful, and life has everything in store for you. You're so young...so much has yet to happen."

I bite my lip. "Yeah, I suppose. But what happens when I'm old? What then?"

"Just cling to that youth, honey. Hang on to it as long as you can. Look at me, pushing forty-two and I still look like a schoolgirl." She winks and turns. I listen to her heels clicking on the hardwood and then the click of the door as it closes.

In a moment, though, the door creaks back open. "Gary!"

Heavily, I get up and go to the entranceway to the kitchen, where I can see Henrietta, head poked in the front door.

"Tonight we're going out clubbing. We'll dance our asses off to her memory." She laughs. "I won't take no for an answer."

I nod and whisper, "All right."

After she closes the door, I go over and turn the dead bolt. The hologram is still there, its faint pink glow a contrast to the deep green of the marble below it. I look at it, marveling once more that it has actually changed, transformed itself because of something I did. But when I look in the mirror behind it, I still see a very young man, the bloom of his youth untouched.

And I realize something—it *is* the portrait that will change, it *is* the portrait that will grow old instead of me. My wish on that day that now seems so far off, when I offered to give my soul to have the portrait grow old while I stayed young and handsome, has come true. I realize something else—this will be a fascinating process to watch.

I am blessed.

Chapter Fourteen

LIAM

He would be inconsolable, I was certain. I hurried up Lake Shore Drive, pace brisk, on a mission of mercy. I had seen the news yesterday in a late edition of the *Chicago Tribune* and was stunned by Zoe D'Angelo's passing, even more stunned to read it had been by her own hand and in such an untidy and violent manner.

I had tried calling Gary throughout the day and into the evening. At night, when I phoned and listened to those distant rings, uninterrupted even by his mechanical voice on the answering machine, I began to picture him alone in his high-rise apartment, despairing, sitting in the dark. I had known grief once or twice in my own life, but I wasn't sure if I had ever felt it as intensely as he must have been feeling it. To be so in love, so consumed by infatuation, and to have that cut short by such a final loss must have been horrible. So horrible, in fact, that I began to worry that Gary might try to follow his Zoe down the same path. I had tried Henrietta at home, knowing that she'd been off the previous night. Brian told me she had gone out clubbing. He didn't know where. He didn't know with whom. He never did. Henrietta could be the most amusing of companions, but compassionate she was not.

This morning, when I had still gotten no answer, I found I was unable to work. I canceled a job I had and decided there would be no relief from my worry unless I saw Gary for myself. I didn't let myself believe with any depth that he had done something as rash as taken his own life, but I knew this was no time for him to be alone. If necessary, I would bring him home with me and nurse his broken heart.

In the marbled tile foyer of his lobby, I found the doorman.

"Good morning, sir. What can I do for you?"

"Could you call Gary Adrion for me? He's in 3802."

"Certainly."

With a slightly jittery feeling, I watched as the man punched in the numbers on the switchboard, staring at his expectant face as he listened to the ringing. If Gary didn't answer, I was ready to confess my fears and insist that someone accompany me upstairs to check on him. But I didn't have to use that plan.

"Yes, sir," the doorman said, "there's a Mr....?" The doorman looked at me, questioning.

"Howard."

"A Mr. Howard here to see you."

"Okay." The doorman hung up the phone and smiled. "He says to go right on up. Just take the elevators to your left."

"Thank you." I hurried toward the copper doors, relieved to know that Gary had at last answered his own phone. Relieved to know he was still able.

When Gary answered the door, I was surprised. He greeted me with a smile that lit up his face. He was slightly flushed, and his eyes twinkled.

Oh God, I thought. *What have I gotten myself into? He doesn't know. He doesn't know.*

"Hello, Gary." I tried to smile myself, but the suspense of knowing I would have to deliver some very bad news to him weighed heavily. I dreaded having to face his sorrow. I didn't wait for an invitation to come in but passed into his apartment and looked around. Everything seemed in order, untouched by grief. There were no empty glasses or overflowing ashtrays, just the sun shining brightly on Gary's white leather couch and chairs. "How are you?"

He smiled, and I thought again, a bit ashamed of myself, how absolutely stunning this young man was.

"I'm fine, Liam." He cocked his head. "This is an unexpected surprise."

"I... I just wanted to see you," I stammered.

"Well, here I am. A little worse for the wear, though. Last night Henrietta took me on what she called a pub crawl. I didn't get in until after four. She sure knows how to party." He laughed. "And I have the headache to prove it."

The job of breaking the news would fall on me. I hoped I could do it delicately enough. I bit my lip. "You don't know, do you?"

"What do you mean? Do you want some coffee? I just made some."

"Not right now. Why don't you sit down."

Gary collapsed into one of his leather armchairs and put his feet up on the matching ottoman, lit a cigarette, and directed a plume of blue smoke at the ceiling.

I crossed to the window and looked at the skyline to the south, took a few deep breaths, then turned. "Gary, night before last, Zoe D'Angelo committed suicide." I watched his reaction. The smile vanished from his face, and yet it didn't seem he was overly horrified. He looked serious but not broken up. I supposed shock could have lessened the severity of his initial reaction.

"I know," he said. "Henrietta came over here yesterday morning to break the news."

I closed my eyes with relief. *At least he knows.* And then the alarm began to stir inside. "Did you hear me? Zoe D'Angelo has killed herself."

He nodded. "I know."

I started to feel the anger stirring within me. "Well then, I don't understand. You said you were out dancing and drinking until dawn last night with Henrietta."

Gary laughed. "It was good medicine. She knew what I needed."

My voice rose without my having any conscious intention of it. "I don't get it! How could you be out on the same day you just found out the love of your life killed herself?" I paused. "Have you been down to see her mother, at least?" Gary had told me how close Zoe was to her mother. Any decent person would have gone to offer his sympathy.

"No. I don't see why I should."

"Because she's lost her only daughter! Have you lost your mind?"

"What good would it do for me to go down there and hold her hand? She barely knew me."

I almost choked on my words, as if I could find the right words in the first place. My thoughts were of that poor girl, lying in an alley, lovely face burned by chemicals. And just a few hours later, her love, the man who had probably caused her to feel desperate enough to take her own life, was out dancing. Had I misjudged him? Could this be the Gary I had grown so infatuated with? It wasn't just his beauty that drew me to him, but the air of essential goodness and innocence he seemed to carry with him.

"You were her fiancé, Gary. Didn't you think it was your place?"

"The woman didn't even know my name."

"What?"

"Zoe always referred to me as Prince Charming." He chuckled, and the little laugh filled me with horror. "I just don't think there would be much I could do for her."

I shook my head. "I can't believe you. How could you go out dancing?"

"She was dead, Liam. Staying in and moping wouldn't have changed a thing."

"Moping?" I flailed around, trying to find words to adequately convey my outrage. "Moping? Gary, the girl is dead!"

"I know that."

"There are horrors in store for that little body of hers!"

Gary stood. "Oh, don't be so melodramatic. You sound like some kind of Victorian novel." He started toward the kitchen. "I'm getting some coffee. Do you want some or not?"

I grabbed his shoulder with a savagery I didn't know I possessed. "No! No, I don't want coffee! I want to understand how the day after this horrible thing you can be so calm."

"Henrietta was wonderful support. She helped me talk through it. I'm okay now. The past is the past, Liam."

"What are you talking about? Two days ago? That's the past?"

"The actual lapse of time has nothing to do with it." Anger flared now in Gary's eyes. "Who are you to decide what's an appropriate amount of time for grief?"

I stared at the window, listening to Gary in the kitchen, the creak of a cupboard opening, the ceramic mug on the tile of his counter, the liquid rush of the coffee being poured into a cup. I couldn't believe this. Where was the innocent boy I had photographed just a few weeks ago? Had Henrietta already corrupted him this thoroughly? For a moment I hated her.

He came back into the room. "Listen, Liam, don't look so upset. You came here, I think, to comfort me, right?"

"Of course I did."

"Well, I'm okay. So you should be satisfied. It's like most do-gooders. They aren't really satisfied unless what they're railing against is there. When it's gone, there's nothing for them to do."

"What?"

"You came here to comfort me, to make me feel better. So... I do. And you can't stand it because now your job has been taken away."

"Oh, that's garbage."

"I don't think it is. Just be glad I'm not sitting around here all depressed."

I closed my eyes to try to shut out the pain of what I was hearing, knowing that, in a way, Gary was right. Finally, "Okay... I won't bring up the subject again."

"Thank you."

I thought the best thing to do now would be change the subject. "I've been wondering if you wouldn't do me the honor of sitting for me again." I was shocked by the emotion that washed over his features. He almost seemed terrified.

He shook his head. "Absolutely not. Never. Is that clear?"

I laughed, but there was no humor in it. Gary was drifting away. I was completely at odds to explain his behavior to myself. "But I have a gallery show, and I thought..."

"It isn't happening, Liam!" Gary turned his back on me to stare out the window.

"All right, all right." I held up a placating palm. I never would have guessed Gary would be so much against the idea. "I can at least use the one I've already done, then. That's not a problem, is it?"

Gary lit another cigarette. "No way."

"I don't understand you."

"There's nothing to understand. I don't want to do it again." Gary thought for a moment, then asked, "I've always been curious. Why didn't you want to display the other hologram in the first place?"

For so long, I had dreaded that question. Even now I wasn't sure I could answer it. I felt a flush rise to my face, so hot it made me pull at my collar. "Never mind."

"No, I really want to know. You said it was your finest work, if I recall."

I took a deep breath, genuinely sorry I had canceled my appointment for this morning. How much easier life would have been had I simply not come over here today. "Because sometimes a work of art can reveal more about the artist than it does about his subject."

Gary nodded. "I don't get it."

I bit my lip, unsure if I should tell him. What the hell? It was no secret I was fascinated with him...more. "It shows too much. Anyone looking at that glorious work of art—" I laughed. "—would know that the artist was hopelessly in love with his subject."

Gary stared at me. Then a smile turned up the corners of his mouth. Was it derision? I pushed the thought out of my mind, forcing myself to believe Gary could never be that cruel.

"That's sweet."

"Oh, shut up." I smiled, feeling as if I wanted to be anywhere but there. A line of sweat had formed at my hairline, and I angrily wiped it away. "The portrait is probably so good because I was so completely in awe of the subject. There...are you satisfied?"

"I wasn't looking for satisfaction. I just want us to be friends again."

"We never stopped."

"So we'll still see each other."

"I'll see you whenever you want. You know that." I gathered up the navy blue windbreaker I had left on the back of a chair with trembling hands. "You and Henrietta," I began, hating myself already for what I was about to say, "seem to have become quite chummy. I wonder if she doesn't fulfill all your needs for friendship."

"You mean do I like her better than you?"

"Wipe that smirk off your face! Yes, yes! That's what I mean."

Gary crossed the room and took my face in his big hands. "No one could ever replace you. Henrietta's fun...but you're my best friend. You always will be."

I bit my lip, staring hard at the floor. His touch had aroused me...and somehow I thought he might catch on. I felt a conflicting mixture of emotions—humiliation, excitement, relief, joy, despair. "I should be going," I stammered.

"You will keep in touch?"

"Always. Take care of yourself." I hurried out of his apartment without looking back.

Chapter Fifteen

GARY

After Liam made his request to display the hologram, I knew it wouldn't be long before he'd insist I let him see it. I could just imagine it on a pedestal in some white-walled, recess-lit gallery somewhere, with little gaggles of patrons clustering around it. One would say, "Look at the mouth… That's a mean son of a bitch." And then, by chance, they would see the subject of the portrait somewhere. They would wonder what tricks the artist used to alter my countenance…and would wonder why. That same patron might say, "Why, the model was just a boy. Why would the artist *choose* to take his innocence away? What was the point?" People would speculate. And the hologram would become a kind of curiosity, because the next time they saw it, it would look different from the last.

It must be hidden. There's no other way to avoid the questions Liam would ask. He, of all people, would notice the difference immediately. At least, if the hologram turns up "missing," I can claim ignorance when he asks to see it. It would hurt Liam's feelings, the fact that I didn't know where the work he had put so much time and effort into was, but he would live with that oversight much more easily than he would live with the fact that his masterpiece had somehow transformed itself in the weeks since he had created it.

The larger apartments in my building all come with a fairly good-sized storage room in the basement. The added space might seem like an amenity until one ventures down there. The high-rise I live in, just a little north of Belmont, is one of the older ones, a skyscraper when it was built in the 1940s, now mostly dwarfed by its neighbors. The point I'm trying to make is this—our basement is no clean, well-lighted place. It's the stuff of horror movies. Dingy, the shadows reign down there, only feebly challenged by the irregularly spaced bare light bulbs. When you go down there, you feel alone, in spite of sounds like pipes jangling and elevators humming. Rather than making you feel more a part of the world of people, hearing these sounds, dim and muffled, makes you feel isolated, cut off. No human voice, however, penetrates the gloom. Nor does any light. The windows that do exist are situated high, near the ceiling, which is a network of insulation-shrouded pipes and copper tubing. They let in no light, just a murky gray that filters in through the dirty opaque glass, fronted with metal grating.

I don't like to go down there. Of course, the Freddie Krueger scariness of the place is one reason. But the other reason, the larger of the two, I suppose, is the fact that the basement storage room holds my past. When I attained my twenty-first birthday, I made sure all vestiges of my childhood were taken there, neatly catalogued on shelves...and forgotten. The first two parts of my plan were easy to achieve. My cleaning lady took care of that. But the forgetting is something I still have trouble doing. If I leave my growing up behind in my daily conscious thoughts, it is there in my nightmares, horrid dreams that I waken from sweating, still enraged. Most dreams concern my grandfather, who raised me and provided every conceivable luxury, except warmth and affection. In these dreams, I scream at him, tears flowing, all the emotions I never dared speak of when I was growing up fully venting.

And now all traces of him and the cold existence he made my childhood are down there. Family photographs, the objets d'art I took from his house when he died—a Ming vase, Waterford crystal, a real LeRoy Neiman, various rare books on military history that the old man collected. I wanted none of these things...but his hold on me was strong enough for me to think of giving them away or selling them as heresy.

I listen to the hum of the elevator now as I descend, the distant chime as we pass yet another floor. Amazing how fast twenty-odd floors can go by. When I get to the lobby, I will have to change to the freight elevator. Fitting to dispense with the copper and marble walls and take second-rate transport, an appropriate introduction to the basement.

I have brought my own flashlight to penetrate the gloom. As well maintained as the building is, one can still hear the shrieking of rats, vague whispers of movement that let me know I'm not alone. It is cold down here, and I wish I wasn't carrying the bulky box that holds the hologram so I could wrap my arms around myself.

I pass a row of old washing machines, long out of use, cobwebs clouding their control panels. I try not to breathe too deeply the musty smell in the air. A left up ahead and I will be at my own storage space. Before I came down, I made sure I had the key. I come down here, naturally, as little as possible, and if I forgot something and had to go back, I wasn't sure how long it would be before I could force myself to return.

My footfalls on the concrete floor sound desperate and alone. They remind me, much like the souvenirs waiting inside the storage room, of my childhood. Grandfather, as he insisted on being called, brought me up with staff and private tutors. I never had the privilege of going to public or private institutions of learning. Never went to a high school dance or a football game, never even had a girlfriend. An image of Zoe D'Angelo rises up before me, making me nauseated, and a hot flush of shame spreads down from my hairline and up from my chest, reminding me of my real purpose in coming down here.

For a moment a horrible image, completely unbidden, appears. I imagine rounding the final corner to my storage room and seeing Zoe waiting. Even though I hadn't seen the corpse, I could imagine her lovely face scarred by the chemicals, the blood and mucus draining from her nose and ears, standing with her head lolling on her broken neck like a macabre Jill-in-the-box.

I shake my head to clear it and pick up my pace. The storage room is just ahead. I take my key from my pocket.

Inside, the room is cool, and I pause in the doorway for just a moment before clicking on the light. Dust seems to surround me, diving for my nose and eyes. I sneeze. Today I am plagued with imagination, turning on the lights and seeing Grandfather sitting there, eyes vanished from his sockets, grinning, liver-spotted hands beckoning...

I turn the lights on. Nothing but a long table and rows of cupboards. I should send Helena, the woman who cleans for me, down here to dust occasionally. Everything is thick with it, and cobwebs hang ghostly from the pipes above my head. I move to the long table and set the box down on it.

I stop.

My original intention was just to leave the thing down here, in its box. Even if someone other than myself came into the room, they wouldn't see the hologram. But something pulls on me...a compulsion, I guess. I find myself opening the box, lifting out the glass dome and the equipment that will bring me to life.

I have to see it once more, even though a part of me says not to.

The lips, thinned by cruelty, are still there. And I can still recall my half smile, lips open to reveal my teeth. It isn't my imagination. That's the way it is. I feel a chill run up my spine, icy fingers touching lightly, as I wonder how something like this could possibly occur.

I have never been one to traffic in the supernatural, leaving all that for the *X-Files* and *Unsolved Mysteries* crowd. Fox network devotees. But a hologram, with its kind of ephemeral solidity, changing on its own, the evidence right here before me, cannot be denied. And I can't help but recall that bright August day when I promised to give anything if only the portrait would age instead of me. And now it appears my wish is coming true. What will it be like in five, ten years, as I head down the road toward middle age? Will I really stay the same? Will people whisper and nudge each other, the words "plastic surgery" on their envious lips? It will be fascinating to watch the changes in the hologram as the years pass, fascinating to see it marred by crow's-feet, graying, thinning hair, the inevitable sag of my jowls. Somehow the excitement of seeing that is marred by the reality of the fact that I promised something in exchange for the granting of my wish. What dark force has claimed my soul? Will the currency I dealt in one day prove horribly expensive?

I force myself to look away from the little pink-tinged figure beneath the dome, in spite of its almost magnetic pull. The very freakishness of it draws me back, as if it's some sort of sideshow curiosity.

I rummage through the boxes and find what I have in mind—a purple-and-white scarf, still soft to the touch, one of the only remnants I have of a mother I never knew. I hold the scarf to my cheek for a moment, feeling its cool smoothness, then move it to my nose, a thing I've done many times in the past, always disappointed because there is no vestige of her there, no lingering smell.

I shroud the hologram's dome and resist the urge to pull the scarf away and look once more.

In the box are other remnants of my long-departed parents—a stack of letters, ivory cream linen stationery, tied with a crumbling red ribbon, that detailed my parents' brief love affair, their longing for one another, their desires for a future they would never have.

And there is the mallet. I pick it up, testing its heft. Grandfather never had much use for tools, but this was always around, frightening me as a child. He kept it on a table in his bedside. I suppose it was his protection, the way some people keep a baseball bat in the bedroom. The mallet, with its gray solidity, looks particularly menacing here in the stark, dull light of the bare lightbulb above me. Some of the wood has been chipped away, the scars in its oak handle deep.

Nothing is permanent.

The shrouded hologram seems to mock me, as if something breathing is under the silk, daring me to look once more. Its pull is difficult to deny. I whisper to myself that I have done the job I came down here to do, and I set the mallet back on the long table and hurry from the room.

Back upstairs, the day has turned dark. A gray sky, the color of curdled milk, presses close to my windows. A life of leisure, I think and laugh, is what my grandfather left me, this legacy of a trust fund that requires I do nothing. I look around the living room, bored. So much has happened this week, and now everything has come to an end.

On top of the shelves that house my television and stereo equipment is a disc Henrietta left for me the last time she was here.

"You'll enjoy this, honey. It's fucking weird."

I open the case and free the disc from its plastic sheath. There is no writing on it, save for the Sony logo and a few lines for someone to write in what it's all about. But these lines have been left blank.

I pop the disc in and sink down into an overstuffed chair of white leather. I'm very tired, as if all the events that have taken place have suddenly caught up to me, fingers of fatigue working their way into the deepest parts of my being. I lift my legs up on the ottoman and rest my head on the back of the chair, knowing whatever is on the disc will have to be very gripping to keep me awake.

As the credits, in French, begin, I see that this is an old movie, black and white, with a kind of minimalist music soundtrack, something from Philip Glass perhaps, but too early for him. Strange, discordant notes seep from the stereo speakers.

I watch, mesmerized. This is no ordinary film. I suppose one might say it is of the expressionist school. The strange music continues to play as the screen is awash with images from a young man's life. There is sex. There is death that looks too dull, giving it an unvarnished reality. The film seems to tell the tale of a young man who is learning to experience his life though the senses...taste, touch, smell. Henrietta's saying comes back to me, "To cure the senses by means of the soul and the soul by means of the senses."

I wonder why she gave this to me. In spite of her pointed tongue and her wit, here in the Midwest referred to as "sarcasm," Henrietta is a very perceptive girl. There are parallels in my life with the young man on the screen. He even looks something like me, drinking in the world around him with a kind of wide-eyed wonder.

And I begin to see that this *is* my life...a life of the senses. I will, because of my unending youth, be able to experience what others, whose mortal bodies thicken and fail, cannot.

The film is disturbing, saying volumes about ennui and despair, the emptiness of this life, but I know it's what I will do, how I will live my life. It's ahead of me, waiting, a course I will follow...finding and experiencing everything life has to offer with no repercussions. Let the hologram bear those.

My head sags, images of dream merging with screen images. I close my eyes and finally sleep.

Chapter Sixteen

HENRIETTA

"Honey, you need some night life," I argued into the phone to Mr. Gary Adrion. He had been cold and distant for almost a month, and I was sick of it. Wouldn't come out with me, wouldn't see Liam. Lord knows what he was doing, shut up in that bought-and-paid-for condo on Lake Shore Drive. Weeping tears for lost love, maybe. But wait, that didn't seem likely, because he went out the night after that Isadora Duncan of his offed herself.

"So what do you say, sugar? Wanna date?" I asked seductively, in the dulcet tones of a hooker. That got a laugh out of him.

"I suppose I could come out for one or two."

"One or two what? Because, honey, you can have both of mine!"

I was on a roll. He laughed again.

"I'll pick you up around ten. Think you can be ready— Wait a minute! Listen to me! Honey, you're ready if you just rolled out of bed. Sleep in your eyes and your hair sticking out in several different directions, you'd still be the hottest stud in the place."

"Go on, Henrietta," he said with a chuckle and I thought *I'm a regular Florence Nightingale for the soul.* "You're too nice to me."

"Don't pull that modesty shit with me. It's unbecoming when someone looks like you. The only people who complain about their looks are the gorgeous ones. The others don't want to hear the truth."

"Ten o'clock, then?"

"Be waiting for me in the lobby. If someone has to be kept waiting, it should be the gentleman."

*

I imagined myself quite the glamorous figure as I roared up the circular drive in front of Gary's building. Little red sports car and me, emerging from it like some fucked-up, armed Venus de Milo. Let me just tell you, sugars, how good I looked, fire-engine-red stiletto heels—four inches, and that makes me an Amazon—seamed black silk hose, a tight little Versace spangled red tube dress, and a big black upsweep. I would dwarf Michael Jordan. I am *serious*!

I loved it! I just loved it when I walked up to the doorman to ask for Gary. He gave me the once-over in a major way, almost as if he was deciding what he should do. He picked up the phone and punched in Gary's number.

"He says to go on up."

The doorman, a fat blond with a few wispy hairs poking out from under his green uniform cap, looked at me briefly, then stared down at his marble desk. When I embarrassed someone, it just made me want to try all that much harder to keep the face-reddening tactics up. I placed a hand over his and squeezed. He pulled away and looked up, alarmed. I winked.

"Thanks, sugar." I sashayed off toward the elevators.

*

It had been a couple of months since I'd been there. In that time, summer's heat had faded to autumn, and even in the yellow glare cast by the streetlights, I could see the leaves already putting out their finest colors in Lincoln Park from Gary's windows.

A change had come over the apartment too. We're talking drastic here. I gave a low whistle. "Goddamn! Someone's been making the charge card smoke." The place had been completely redone. Where once a kind of comfortable contemporary look had reigned, there was now a more stately aspect.

Gary smiled. As usual, he looked good enough to eat, even though he was wearing only a pair of tight black jeans, a white banded-collar shirt, and a black suede vest. The severity of the lack of color and the vertical lines of his clothes made his body appear even more perfect than usual. His complexion was ruddy, and those aquamarine eyes that made my knees turn to water sparkled.

"I've been haunting the antique stores."

"I'll say. Must be nice." I ran my hand lovingly along the paisley pattern of his new couch. One thing this girl knew when she saw it was quality, and quality reigned here. It was some sort of wonderful mixture of Chippendale and Louis XIV...lots of mahogany, brass, and fussy overstuffed chairs covered in satin. "You've got a whole new look goin' on."

"I do." He beamed. Gary moved to the fireplace, above which hung a small impressionist painting of a field with red poppies. "Monet."

"Is that real?"

"Oh yes. I figured I might as well use some of my trust fund to invest. I've been buying a lot of things lately...art, rare books..."

He cocked his head to a glass-fronted bookcase in the corner of the room, made from mahogany. Inside, each shelf was filled with leather-bound volumes. I wanted to stay and peruse the titles, but an urge to dance pulled me.

"I've got to come over here and check things out more thoroughly, but tonight is not the night for that."

*

We arrived at Angst about eleven thirty. There was still breathing room in the cavernous dance club, but it had begun filling up with the usual assortment of club kids, Goth chicks, and wannabe bikers. You could smell the leather! A fog machine was sending out rolls of gray smoke across the dance floor, a huge raised platform under a four-story-high ceiling that boasted a network of pulsating lights, heating ducts, and pipes painted cobalt blue, chartreuse, and yellow. Bottles of Evian and Pellegrino were everywhere, giving ready evidence that the revelers had already started in on the mood enhancers—X, K, crystal... It would be boisterous tonight, and by 2:00 a.m. the dance floor would be so crowded Gary and I would be lucky to move.

"What do you want?"

I eyed Gary up and down, grinning.

"Cut it out! What do you want to drink?"

"I think I'll start with something sweet and fruity"—I cocked my head coquettishly—"like me." Gary rolled his eyes. "Just bring me a fuckin' daiquiri...lime."

"Coming right up."

Gary weaved through the crowd, and along with watching his tight ass, I also watched the crowd part and the heads, both male and female, swivel as he walked by.

*

My prediction was right. By two o'clock Gary and I were surrounded by revelers. Most of the men were shirtless now, including Gary, and the muscles shifting around me like tectonic plates made my heart faint. All the men's chests were hairless. Whether they were that way naturally or not I couldn't tell, save for a closer, hands-on inspection. The women continued bobbing and weaving, chains and crucifixes clacking, their makeup beginning to run. The club would close in a couple of hours, and the predatory glances were already beginning.

"Excuse me," a voice whispered loudly behind me, accompanied by a tap on my shoulder. I turned to see a little girl. Really, her small size and waifish face made her look about ten years old. She cocked her head. "I've only seen this in the movies," she said, straining on tiptoes to speak into my ear, or as close as she could get to it, "but would you mind if I cut in?"

My mouth dropped open, speechless. *Nobody* cuts in on Miss Henrietta, and I was just about to read this little bitch when I felt Gary's hand on my arm. I looked up at him, stunned, and he was smiling. "Would it be okay?" he mouthed. I took one last glance at the little tramp and, disgusted, headed for the bar.

After getting myself another libation, I stood at the edge of the dance floor and watched them. The girl, as I said, looked almost prepubescent in her little black dress and high heels...like she was playing dress-up. Her head was topped with a shock of blonde hair that stood up in spikes. She wore a tiny gold hoop in one nostril, and a row of hoops in a line, five or six, trailing up one ear. She had big dark eyes and cheekbones I could discern from over here, even with the fog and the flashing multicolored lights. She was beautiful in a way I would never be. Envy is the province of the pathetic, but I had to admit I would give a lot to look like she did, youth and beauty and *femininity*.

It seemed as if the two of them danced for hours. When they finally rolled up to me, I pretended to be miffed, but there was a part of me that was happy for Gary. I had never seen him, well, cut loose quite like this before.

They were both panting, and Gary took big swigs from the girl's water bottle. "This is Lucinda," he said, gesturing toward her. "And this is my best friend, Henrietta."

She held out a tiny hand, and I grabbed her fingertips for a quick shake. Her hand in mine looked like the giant and the princess. Honey, sometimes the truth makes you ache. "Charmed," I said.

She smiled, revealing rows of perfect white teeth and, Christ, dimples.

"Lucinda knows about an after-hours party and wondered if we'd like to go."

I knew about these after-hours and wondered if our innocent Mr. Adrion was ready for such a scene, which usually culminated in an orgy of flesh and chemicals. "You wanna go?"

"Very much." He glanced down at Lucinda. I saw him grab her hand and squeeze. I felt like the maiden aunt and considered not going, but that flew out the window, along with any protective instincts toward Gary.

"I'd love to go. Where are we headed?"

*

The Wicker Park loft was a big place, converted from what I suppose was an old warehouse. The walls were exposed brick, the floor concrete, and all around were huge windows protected by wire mesh. A spiral staircase stood in the middle of the big room like some sort of black metal and hardwood centerpiece. I was staring up at it, a bottle of Evian in my hand, when someone approached me.

"It leads up to a rooftop deck."

I turned to see a negative image of Gary...almost as handsome but black. Green eyes stared out of his light-shaded chocolate complexion, and a thin mustache and goatee lined his mouth.

"I'm Cyril," he said, extending his hand. "This is my place."

"Cyril? Really? You have to meet my friend Liam just so you two can bemoan your names."

Cyril laughed, rubbing his goatee with one hand. "And who are you?"

"Henrietta Wotton."

"Do you perform down at the Façade?"

I was both charmed by the recognition and horrified. When I met a man I liked—and who could resist this one, with his perfect physique shown off by a rubber tank top and tight, worn Levi's?—I liked to keep the illusion going as long as I could. Smoke and mirrors, honey, smoke and mirrors. But what the hell. He knew. "Yes, I am a headliner at that dubious establishment."

He chuckled again. "You're a trip."

His voice was a rich, deep baritone that put me in mind, I swear, of Barry White. It made me want to laugh out loud and wrap my legs around him. I have always been a complex mixture of emotions.

He nodded upward, gesturing toward the spiral staircase. "If you think you and your spike heels can make it, there's a gorgeous view of the city from up there. You can see the whole skyline to the east."

I bent and slipped out of my shoes. "Now we don't have to worry, baby. Let's go." About halfway up the stairs, I turned to see what Gary was up to. I found him, after a seconds-long search, in a corner of the room on one of several big couches, Lucinda spread-eagled on his lap and facing him. At least they still had their clothes on. I felt Cyril's hand on my butt.

"C'mon, sugar, you don't need to worry about anyone." He paused. "Except for me."

I liked this one.

*

Cyril and I were on the rooftop for more than two hours. By the time we came back down, the sky was beginning to lighten in the east...a dull gray-lavender that brought form and definition to the quiet streets of Wicker Park below us. The sun was throwing out a few bars of gold behind the silhouetted backdrop of Chicago's skyline.

Cyril had proved to be quite the aggressive soul and before long had unburdened me of both dress and stockings. He was the kind of man I liked...confident enough in his own masculinity to let a drag queen fuck him up the ass. I giggled as I thought of him biting down on a pillow atop an old futon I supposed had been put up on the deck for the sole purpose of sex and nude sunbathing. Since the sun was down...

Leaving Cyril sore and snoring behind me, I crept down the stairs, wondering how our innocent Gary was faring for himself. It was dark in the loft, dim gray light filtering in through slats from miniblinds that had been lowered while Cyril and I had our alfresco rendezvous. But Miss Henrietta knew the sounds of lovemaking...the grunts, groans, and sighs of pleasure were heavily in evidence. The floor was strewn with bodies, like some sort of carnal battlefield. I could see movement.

But I couldn't see Gary. I made my way through the crowd, feeling the occasional hand grab at my leg, trying to pull me down. I wished I could remember where I left my shoes so I could kick at those impertinent digits.

Gary was nowhere. Had that fool gone off and left me there to fend for myself? He would be read when I got ahold of him!

A block of yellow light outlined what I supposed was the kitchen, which had been partitioned off from the rest of the loft by drywall. As I drew closer to the light, I smelled something familiar, the acrid chemical smoke of cooking cocaine.

In the kitchen, Gary was wide-eyed on a ladder-back chair. Lucinda was at the stove, a spoon in her hand. White liquid bubbled in the tablespoon.

I shook my head, knowing what she was doing, being a refugee from my earlier, more addlebrained druggie days. I slipped back into the shadows to watch the new couple.

Lucinda took the liquid from the stove and dumped it onto a mirror lying on the kitchen table. Her small hands picked up a razor blade once the stuff had cooled down and chopped and slid the powdery substance around until there were several tiny pebbles of hard white powder. She scooped these into a glass pipe. Guess our boy was growing up.

She gave Gary the pipe first, and he lit it. I watched as a cloud of smoke formed like magic inside the glass and then just as magically disappeared when he inhaled. He smiled and handed the pipe back to Lucinda.

She took her fill and then knelt between Gary's legs. She licked the fabric of his jeans until they were wet and then, with her tongue, tugged at his zipper.

I felt I shouldn't be watching, but there was no way I was turning away from this. I wanted to see if Mr. Adrion was as magnificent in all areas as he was in what he put on everyday display.

He was. A purple-veined penis, at least eight inches long, popped up from the fabric. I covered my mouth with my hand. Lucinda swallowed him down to the root, and his head went back. He sighed.

Lucinda's tube dress had slid up to her belly, and I could see her hand working furiously between her legs as she treated Gary to what I could tell was her very experienced mouth. I moved a little more to my left and gasped. What she was working between those legs was easily as big as what Gary had between his. Good God! And I, the supposed acknowledged expert on drag queens, had never even guessed this tiny creature's secret. I had to give her credit.

I moved back more into the shadows and bumped into several other bodies who had gathered to watch the performance of Fellatio in E minor by the virtuoso Lucinda.

We all watched, none of us moving or making a sound, as Lucinda, with her expert lips and tongue, brought our Mr. Adrion to new heights of dubious pleasure.

I guess the innocence I had once ascribed to him had up and flown the coop. Ah well, it happens to us all sooner or later. And Gary was ripe for knowledge.

I had a feeling this was just the beginning of Gary's trip down the long road to hedonistic discovery.

I knew Liam would not approve.

Chapter Seventeen

LIAM

It was getting close to Christmas. I had been too busy to think about the holidays, which was just as well. Although I had scores of "friends" from my business, which resulted in my mailbox overflowing with party invitations, there weren't really that many people who could make the holiday special. Having a gallery show and two major corporate jobs—a brochure for an Internet provider and the annual report for a Fortune 500 food products company—kept me going all day long, until I collapsed into bed. I hadn't been able to give much thought to Gary Adrion and, truth be told, hadn't laid eyes on the young man in several months. But that didn't mean I hadn't heard about him.

Henrietta had called earlier in the afternoon. "Is this Liam Howard?" she asked, and I wondered what was coming.

"You know it is, Henrietta."

"So you are still breathing?"

I rolled my eyes. "Yes, Henrietta. I'm sorry I haven't been in touch, but things have just been ridiculously hectic. They always are this time of year."

"Yes, old Liam's making piles of money, I'm sure. But he's being shortchanged in the time department. In the end, I wonder which he'll think is more valuable."

"Did you call for a reason? Or are you about to launch into a lecture about how I should get out more? Perhaps tell me that my work will, in the end, amount to nothing?"

Henrietta tittered. "I just wanted to see if I could have the pleasure of His Excellency's company for an hour or two. A cup of coffee and two girls gossiping."

"Oh, Henrietta." From the day I met her, I had a love-hate relationship with the camp behavior. It both charmed and repelled. Right now, it repelled.

"I won't take no for an answer."

I glanced at my calendar and saw that I *would* be free after six. "How about six o'clock?"

"Nervous Center?"

"Fine."

*

By six o'clock that night, the snow was coming down heavily, traffic was in a snarl, and the winds were whistling down alleys and over the tops of buildings, throwing needles of frozen precipitation into the faces of those unlucky enough to be outside.

Henrietta was already at the Nervous Center, seated on an old gray flannel couch near the back. She had dressed down, remarkably, wearing a pair of jeans and a sweatshirt. Of course, there were some concessions to glamour, as she might have called it. A gold pendant around her neck, big gold hoops in her ears, and a pair of totally inappropriate black high heels.

"What are you doing wearing those shoes? You'll break your neck."

"And hello to you, too, stranger. Gee, I've been missing you as well." Henrietta rolled her eyes.

"I'm sorry." I shrugged out of coat, hat, and muffler. I leaned over and pecked her on the cheek, grabbed her hand, and looked into her golden eyes. "I have missed talking to you. I've pretty much been working from morning until I go to bed at night."

"So I should feel lucky to have the honor of an audience."

I laughed. "Yes, you should." I sat down and ordered an espresso. The two of us chatted about little things for a while—where Brian and Henrietta were going for Christmas (South Beach), where I was going (a vague lie about the home of a friend in the suburbs when the truth was I'd be putting together some new holograms for my next gallery show on Superior Street... It was my new serial killer series and was attracting quite a lot of attention...and controversy), and how the season was becoming so commercial. In short, we wasted breath and said absolutely nothing. But I had to admit, there was a warmth going on. I had really missed the sarcastic bitch's sense of humor and her barbed tongue. Since I was seeing increasingly less of Gary Adrion, Henrietta was the only person I could truly call friend. But there was something else hanging in the air, unnamed, as we made banter, while we were being served our coffee.

I knew what it was. Gary. In the last few months, he had cut a swath through Chicago's party scene. Although I had never been a part of it, having no desire to take part in such empty-headed pleasure, I was still hooked up to the lines that talked about such things, the gallery crowd. And what I heard worried me. People were talking a lot about an extraordinary-looking young man and his appetite for drugs and sex. I had heard that Gary was dealing drugs, chemicals mostly...and he was also known as *the* pipeline to the new drug we were all hearing so much about that winter, a street drug called, simply, Seven. Seven was supposed to contain all the jittery highs of crystal but, with men, seemed to have a Viagra-like effect. Naturally it had become in huge demand, since crystal usually had the contradictory effect of heightening desire while making the power to act on it next to impossible. I don't know what kind of chemicals went into the brew or what its side effects were, but I had heard Gary Adrion was the man to see if you wanted the best.

He was also becoming known as a "debauched intellectual," and while there was a certain cachet to the moniker, a kind of reckless glamour, people spoke of him, I thought, with a kind of discomfort. It was said, and I really don't know how much of what I had heard was true, that he had also become a corrupter of young women...that they were lining up to sample his prodigiously large member and his finesse at the sexual act. The thought of this made me queasy with curiosity, dread, and I must admit, desire. But it wasn't just that. Corny as it sounds, hearts were being broken in the process. And speaking of hearts, people were beginning to wonder if Gary possessed one.

Casually I asked, "Heard from Gary lately?"

Henrietta shook her head. "That boy's on a collision course with disaster. He doesn't tell me much. He knows his auntie wouldn't approve, but I hear things down at the club."

"Like what?"

"Like some people are having second thoughts about hanging out with him. That he's dangerous. That he has a party appetite few can keep up with."

I nodded. "I've heard some of the same things. I suspect you hear more, down at the Façade, plus you've got more of a pipeline into that circuit."

Henrietta lit a cheroot. "I take it all with a grain of salt, baby. Our Gary has led a sheltered life, and he's just cutting loose, sowing some wild oats, if you will. And knowing you, you won't." Henrietta laughed. "Our boy is just ripe for experience..."

"But I hear he's using Seven...and heroin."

"Isn't everybody?"

My mouth dropped open. "Don't look so stunned. It's moved from the derelict element to the party favor of choice these days. Same for Seven." Henrietta struck a haughty pose. "Although I have no need for either."

I didn't think her nonchalance about this matter becoming. "How can you be so casual?"

"I'm not. Gary's just sampling all that life has to offer."

I stared down at the table, which had photographs and headings cut from magazines shellacked into its surface. "Life won't offer much if he keeps going at the rate he's going. Isn't he afraid of AIDS?"

"Aren't we all?" Henrietta directed a plume of smoke at the ceiling. "I wouldn't worry too much about him. He's enjoying his youth."

"I wish he could find other ways. I heard a rumor that Zoe D'Angelo is not the only woman he's driven to suicide."

"I blame no one for suicide except the selfish fool who makes the choice."

I agreed with Henrietta's assessment, but still it pained me to hear the path Gary was taking. It had been a relatively short time since I had met him in an alley near

Belmont, and then he was just an innocent boy. It showed in his bashful smile and the tentative way he had of speaking.

"Gather ye rosebuds while ye may," Henrietta said. "Youth and beauty don't last forever. Gary's just making the most of it. Anyone who's half alive knows the risks for HIV, and if Gary wants to take chances, well, he's a big boy, and I say it's his choice. One does not live forever."

"How can you say that?"

"I can say it because we only have one life.... Gary is simply living his out."

"Heedless of the consequences."

"But at least he has a life."

Henrietta looked pointedly at me, and my mouth dropped open.

"I'm sorry." She took my hand. "But you can't blame Gary for wanting to grab all he can, for exploiting what he has."

"I can and I will." I suddenly wanted to be anywhere but there. I guess when the subject of Gary came up, I had wanted Henrietta to tell me that what I'd heard had all been rumors. That things were not as bad as they seemed.

But as with so much in my life, my hopes were not to be realized. I looked around the Nervous Center, the green sponge-painted walls, the eclectic collection of thrift store furniture and bizarre objets d'art. The counter that was nothing more than a couple of jewelers' display cases, filled with gaudy paperbacks from the 1960s, clippings of bizarre news stories, and a box of human teeth, rumored to have been donated by a prison dentist, who extracted them from murderers.

Henrietta leaned closer. "I heard, and this was from the horse's mouth, honey, that Gary has been banned from the University Club."

"The University Club?"

"Some fancy-shmancy downtown fraternity of old men who make themselves feel better by excluding people. I guess Gary's grandfather was a member and Gary was too, by lineage. He laughed about it when he told me. I told him he should be proud."

I shook my head. I wondered how long Gary's good looks would last, if he were living as roughly as we had heard. Time takes its toll, and when combined with drugs, alcohol, and excess, ruin doesn't take long to show up in the faces of its patrons. "I need to call him. Maybe we can have a quiet Christmas dinner together."

"What about your friends in the suburbs?"

I reddened. I started to stammer out another lie to cover the first, when Henrietta placed a hand over mine. "It's okay. I think you should have him over. One thing about the party set, they're not there for you during times like Christmas."

I nodded.

"Besides, you'll probably stop him from going on some shopping spree. Have you seen his apartment lately?"

I shook my head.

"Honey, he's got a small fortune invested in antiques and artwork. Along with being known as a party boy, he's also getting known to the other kind of dealers around town as quite the patron."

I cocked my head, wondering if Gary realized how empty his life sounded. I said as much.

"Again, Liam, he's just reaching out and grabbing all life has to offer."

"It's hedonistic."

"And what's wrong with that? All we have, sugar, is the present. That much is guaranteed. Nothing else is. I applaud him."

"I don't want to be going to his funeral in a couple of years."

Henrietta pursed her lips, and I suddenly felt like the biggest stick-in-the-mud in town.

"You won't. That boy is charmed."

I gathered up my things and stood. "I need to get going." I leaned over and impulsively kissed Henrietta on the mouth, heedless of the straight patrons at the cafe. Unusual for me. I felt a strange mixture of presentiment and dread.

It seemed as if Gary and I, the both of us, were on a collision course with disaster. I didn't know where it would end.

Chapter Eighteen

GARY

And so the years pass with orderly precision, like dominoes, each falling faster than the last with no discernible pattern, until all the tiles have landed. And who knows when that will be? Who knows if the little bargain I made with the dark forces gathering around me have not only granted me perpetual youth and beauty but immortality as well? It's a daunting thought.

Even though only seven of the tiles have fallen since that fateful day in August when I made a wish I never expected to be granted, it seems longer. So much has happened.

I have become a collector. They know my name at Christie's. I have a nightstand that belonged to Jacqueline Onassis, a small writing table once used by the Windsors, the fedora worn by Humphrey Bogart in *Casablanca*. My apartment is a treasure trove of period furniture, stunning to behold, competition for the wondrous Lake Michigan that roils just outside my apartment windows.

And then there is the music. I have become, apropos of Chicago, a connoisseur of the blues, in more ways than one. My collection boasts rare recordings by Howlin' Wolf, Muddy Waters, and Buddy Guy. I hired Shirley King to sing at my twenty-seventh birthday party. She left long before things got out of hand, which they tend to do at most of my parties.

That night I remember well. You always remember the parties where someone dies.

February. Only last year, but the girl's face is imprinted on my memory, as if her image were carved on the soft pink tissue of my brain with a scalpel. She was Irish, and it showed in her fair skin, her short black hair, and blue eyes that challenged you to look away. Sweet, soft young flesh. I thought at the time, *How sad that this will fade...and then how wonderful she isn't cursed as I am.*

"Great party," she says, sidling up to me after Ms. King has belted out her last number and, with her entourage in tow, is gathering her things to leave. Her voice wrapped around the blues makes me morose in a way I never expected. Already I am beginning to regret my rash wish and starting to feel the effects of it on other people. One man, in his thirties, losing his hair, even had the nerve to ask me, just after the birthday cake was wheeled out, "So who's your plastic surgeon?"

Who's your plastic surgeon? I walked away but wonder how many others had asked the question and how many more would. Envy makes people hateful. How many more years of envy will I have to endure, if the emotion increases proportionally with the years?

"Great party," she says, and I look at her, thinking she can be no more than nineteen or twenty. Already in love with me. I can see it in her eyes. A connoisseur of love, I have seen it many times before. But since Zoe, love is an emotion I seem unable to recapture. I lost that ability when I lost the ability to age.

"One only turns twenty-seven once," I lean over to whisper, and she giggles. Her laugh is like crystal water over rocks, mellifluous, tinkling. It should warm my soul, but it doesn't. "I've never seen you here before. I'm Gary."

She laughs again, and I stiffen, wondering if I will ever be able to laugh so lightheartedly again. The laugh both delights and repels me. It causes a slow-burning anger to form in me, low, an anger born of envy.

"I *know* who you are. I'm Colleen. I've been to a couple of your parties before, and I always wanted to talk to you, but I never had the nerve to approach you."

"Yes, I am a fearsome creature." I roll my eyes.

"Besides, I always had to leave early, so I don't know if the rumors are true."

I pluck a glass of champagne—Dom Perignon 1991—from a tray passing by for each of us. The Baccarat glasses feel cool in my hand, delicate. Colleen sips from hers. "What rumors?" I ask, even though I already know the answer.

"Oh," she says, sipping, "about how wild your parties get. You know..."

I smile. Yes, I do know. My parties have grown infamous around the Windy City, and people clamor for invitations. I could probably sell them, if I needed money. Colleen refers to the fine Mexican heroin I always have on hand, the hashish, the marijuana, almost black, sticky with resin, the pure cocaine...and of course, Seven... Damn the reports of its alarming side effects, which have just begun to show up. I offer a garden of earthly delights...free bliss, all in exchange for a few hours of company.

Or she could be referring to the sex, which my drug-addled revelers always seem to wind up engaging in.

"You haven't missed much. People talk."

Colleen grins at me, engaging me with her ice-blue stare. "I've wanted to meet you for a long time."

I cock my head. "Would you like to sample some of the finest Bolivian cocaine?"

"I've never tried it."

"What? Bolivian?"

She laughs. "No, cocaine. I'm just a green girl from Wisconsin. The wildest I've gotten is downing a six-pack of Budweiser."

"Well, if one is going to be introduced to cocaine, it should be the good stuff and not that cut crap one finds on the street. Are you game?"

There is a hesitancy in her eyes, and I can read it all. I've seen it so many times before. That desire for new experience burning, yet still held in fragile check by fear—of things going too far, of the risks one reads about in newspapers and magazines, the effects one is warned of in school. She takes a second or two to reply. "Well, maybe just a tiny bit."

We disappear into my study, which is the only room I keep locked during my parties. I need a private place to retire to should the need present itself. The girl is beautiful and...untouched. My dick gets hard—Seven is pumping through my system, causing my heart to race and my dick to stay at perpetual half mast, like Caverject and meth all rolled into one—at the prospect of tutoring her in the ways of debauchery. Another eager pupil about to become jaded. How sweet.

We go into the small room, where the only furniture is a Louis XIV mahogany desk and bookcase and a burgundy leather chair. I take out the little plastic baggie of cocaine, which is still in the form of tiny hard rocks.

From a desk drawer, I take out a sterling-silver-backed mirror and pour a little pile of the white powder on its flawless surface. "Pretty, isn't it?"

"Pure as the driven snow," Colleen whispers, casting looks back at the closed and locked door.

"You don't have to stay, you know. There are plenty of others willing to take your place." I watch the girl like a scientist watching a rat in an experiment, waiting to see what she will do. She disappoints me.

"Oh, I wouldn't miss this for the world."

A show of faux confidence. She'll get what she's looking for, all that and more.

I chop up the rocks with a razor blade until all that is left is a mound of fine white powder, which I separate into six equal lines, long and elegant. I take out a crisp ten-dollar bill from my wallet and expertly roll it into a tight tube. I lean over and vacuum up two of them. The sniffing afterward is inelegant, but what are you going to do? I offer her the bill. "Just take your time," I tell her.

She leans over, silken black hair falling over her forehead, and pauses. I watch the indecision with cool detachment. The worst thing I can do is encourage her; she will need to do that for herself. She must not feel she is being coerced. The indecision finally crumbles, and Colleen gets through half the line before she has to stop and catch her breath.

"It's okay," I tell her. White powder adheres to her left nostril, and suddenly she is not so beautiful. "Just take your time."

Eventually, she gets down both lines.

"How do you feel?"

She pauses, listening to herself. "Numb," she says and giggles. But the giggle is more that of an immature schoolgirl. Already I'm growing bored with her.

That night, our Colleen proves an eager pupil. With me, she does line after line, combating the resultant dry mouth with glass after glass of the finest champagne.

I move her to the chair, where I begin to undress her. She cannot stop laughing as her clothes tumble to the hardwood floor, until she is at last naked on my leather chair, legs spread, her pale skin offering contrast to the deep maroon of the chair.

I fuck her, and when she begins to protest as I turn her over to enter her in ways she hadn't imagined, I ignore her and plunge in, feeling her stiffen and cry out, until she goes limp in my arms, breathing shallow, face slick with sweat.

I leave her weeping in my office. "Do some more coke," I say at the door. "It does wonders for the temperament." The last thing I remember seeing of her was the naked body, stooped, heading toward the mirror's glass and the little plastic baggie. Already she knows what to do. Already she's learned that, with cocaine, enough is never enough.

It's not until later, when dawn is creeping into the apartment, that I remember Colleen. As soon as I hear the shriek, followed by a male voice proclaiming, "Oh my God!" I know it's Colleen. I disengage the needle from my arm, already feeling a tinge of heroin's languor, but hurry down the hall.

The door to my study is open, and the light from the room spills into the darkened hallway. Already a crowd of onlookers, kin to those at the Roman coliseum, gather in its entrance, eyes bright with interest.

"Oh my God! Somebody call 911."

"Let me through." I press my way through the crowd and go into my office, where Colleen lies on the floor. Her body twitches. Her eyes are rolled back, and at her nostril, a thin line of crimson drips, bright against her white, white skin.

Snow White.

There is a young man in too-baggy jeans and an oversized T-shirt at my desk telephone. I have never seen him. I walk calmly over to him, looking deep into the almost black orbs of his Latin eyes. I take the phone from his hand, replace it in its cradle. "Get out of here," I say softly to him, but the words convey an inarguable intensity. "I'll take care of this."

I turn. The group of young faces presses in, spilling into the doorway. I realize I have never seen any of them either. "This will be all right," I tell them. "All of you...just go home. The party's over." Reluctantly, they leave. I listen to their hushed conversation, the click of the door as it closes softly behind each of them. Suddenly I hear the music, Vanessa Davis wailing about lost love.

I kneel and pull Colleen close to me, her blood staining my off-white linen slacks. I bite my lip, willing the tears to come, but all I feel are spasms passing through her.

I hold her for a while, until the spasms stop. It's only then that I pick up the phone.

*

After the paramedics have gone, I lie down, fully clothed, on my bed. The sun has risen all the way now, ignorant of what transpired last night in my apartment. Its light streams into the room...a brilliant winter day, the golden light belying the frigid cold outside.

I try to close my eyes and sleep, wanting nothing more than oblivion. How many lives will I ruin? No, I mustn't think that way, but a queasiness rises up when I picture Colleen's fresh young face...a face no one will ever look at again, at least not alive.

"There are horrors in store for that little body of hers!" I can hear Liam saying again. If he only knew...

My muscles twitch, and each time I close my eyes, an invisible hand pulls them open again. Sleep isn't happening...not for a long time, a day or two maybe. I rise from the bed, go to my office, and do a couple of bumps in an attempt to dispel a zombielike lethargy that won't let me sleep but keeps me weighted down, full of fatigue. I sniff and wipe my nose on the back of my hand.

I catch a glimpse of myself in the mirror. I look perfect...as if I've had a good night's sleep, as if my life hasn't been consumed in the relentless hunt for ever-increasing levels of pleasure.

I make a decision. It has been a long time since I've seen the portrait, and I wonder what evidence it will give against me. I hurry into the bedroom, strip out of my clothes, don T-shirt and jeans, and head for the freight elevator.

*

I stand before the shrouded hologram, biting my nails, uncertain if I want to take off the silken scarf that hides the truth. But its pull is magnetic, and I think of a movie tagline I've heard somewhere, fey, but now its meaning is ominous. "Resistance is futile."

The thing pulls at me. I know I will have no peace, no thoughts of anything else unless I complete the course I've taken.

I must look.

Tiredly, even though I'm buzzing inside, I take one corner of the scarf in my hand and slowly draw it away.

Once revealed, I close my eyes before I have a chance to drink in the image before me. Colors swim behind my closed eyelids. I grind my teeth, imagining myself simply turning from the cold storage room and walking away. Back upstairs, to the warmth of my apartment, where I can pop some Xanax and lie down in my canopied bed. Sleep will come.

But if I were that strong a person, I might not be in this situation to begin with.

I open my eyes.

A quivering gasp, like a small trapped bird, flies out of my mouth when I see it. There are, I suppose, tiny signs of age. Perhaps the laugh lines around my mouth have deepened a bit...a few thin lines no one but me would notice across the broad forehead and around the eyes. And the eyes are what grip me most, at first. They are the centerpiece of this grotesque. Even in the pinkish hue, I can see they are filmy, the white not as bright, a yellowish tinge. Broken blood vessels, the first sign of Seven usage, spread over the whites, like veining in marble. The skin has a waxy pallor, a sweaty sheen that indicates fever and not the sweat of the robust. Small, thin scars mar the perfect arms...tracks. Oh God, I wonder, what have I done?

And on my chest, very tiny, really, but there nonetheless, a small dark lesion...looking like a blood blister.

I shudder and turn away from the portrait. I cannot look back. With eyes shut, I pick up the scarf and hide the monster.

Book Two

Chapter Nineteen

GARY

Fog shrouds the streets near Lake Shore Drive. It rolls off the water from the lake, spreading like a virus. It's a little after midnight on the eve of my thirty-eighth birthday. I suppose, more precisely, it *is* my thirty-eighth birthday. Spring around the corner. New beginnings. It's been a new beginning for me now for seventeen years. Or at least to look at my face, that's what one would think. Funny how the new and novel can grow trite and tiresome after a while.

I have tried, these years of my so-called adulthood, not to feel sorry for myself. How many others would kill to be in the position I find myself...perpetual youth and beauty. Ah, what could *you* do with that? It sets the brain synapses to firing, the fantasies to spinning. Isn't it pretty to think so?

I don't want to bemoan my situation. It has opened doors for me, but behind each door lurks a relentless darkness...a darkness, I fear, that would swallow me whole. Yet sometimes the prospect of that is tempting.

Everything tingles this frost-cloaked night. Tonight my veins have been shot full of heroin, my throat has admitted several tabs of Seven, and my nostrils have snorted up crystal meth...all of this washed down with vodka. I have consumed enough drugs and alcohol to kill another man, to at least make of him a withered creature, old beyond his years; yet I live on, robust, red-cheeked, the picture of youthful good health. Did I say picture?

The evening has been spent in revels. My new friends, an artsy crowd of college kids in Wicker Park, have thrown me a huge party, which I suppose raves on even now. It won't run out of steam until tomorrow afternoon.

I always have a steady supply of new friends. Sooner or later, everyone falls away, either from envy or frustration at not being able to figure out my secret. Know me for a few years, and my handsomeness becomes monstrous.

Of course, Henrietta has stood by me. And after a fashion, Liam. I believe they both know my "beauty secret," but it would cause a tad bit too much cognitive dissonance to swallow *that* line whole. Knowledge and acceptance are often two very different things. My "beauty secret" is the kind of thing that happens only in Victorian novels, not in the Chicago of the new millennium. So Henrietta and Liam do what many of us do when presented with mystery, with the inexplicable—ignore it, pretend it isn't there.

My footfalls echo on the pavement. The towers of the city rise above me, and I feel alone. That feeling of singularity, of being one of a kind, follows me these days wherever I go. I am seldom able to forget that I am apart from the rest of the human race. I have plied myself with every kind of drug out there, and yet the best I can hope for is a temporary oblivion. It's quiet here on the Gold Coast. A warm yellow light in a window high up serves only to make me feel less a part of the beehive swarming silently above me. The only sounds are the crash of the waves, the rush of traffic on the drive.

The evening of debauchery and revelry comes back to me in bits and pieces. The partying has left my nerves jangling, a teeth-grinding kind of restlessness that does nothing to combat my despair.

The evening begins with several Glenlivets and a fat joint of the finest Columbian sprayed with PCP. As the music grows louder, the inane comments more frequent, the drugs displayed and consumed, I discover a young girl. Felicity. Fifteen. Freckled. Fair. Two crooked front teeth and short blonde hair. A drug-addled pixie, a Gary Adrion sycophant. I know it from the moment I see her...that familiar awed and adoring look in her eyes. Eyes that are too bright, the pupils dilated, the breathing rapid. The most amusing thing, she assumes I'm but a few years older than she. I slip into a bathroom to run my fingers through my hair and pop a couple of Sevens. Felicity's waiting, and I lead her to a balcony, where we can breathe in the night air, where the wind can sweep over our sweaty bodies, an instant chill. That cold wind causes us to cling together once we're naked and giggling at our foolishness. *Aren't we outrageous?* She gives a little hop, wrapping her legs around me, the heat of her thighs a hot touch to my midsection...clutching, grabbing fistfuls of my hair, so hard it hurts, impaling herself on me.

"You feel wonderful," she gasps, eyes boring right through me.

I grab her hair, too, force her to turn her slack-jawed face to mine, to meet my gaze. "Look at me," I say, the intensity in my voice a command. And yet when her eyes meet mine, she still doesn't see.

"I am looking," she whispers. "Just fuck me."

Sweet words from a girl barely through with playing Barbies. She grinds her hips against me, as if she can't get me inside deep enough...and maybe she can't. Perhaps what she expected to get out of this liaison is unattainable. Her thighs clamp viselike around me, and she moans, desperate.

"Make me come," she whimpers, pushing herself down on me so hard it must hurt. "Make me come, fuck! Make me come." Crying at last, tears hot against my neck.

I turn around, hands supporting the back of her head. Kneeling carefully, not letting go of this tiny doll attached to my body by sweat and her juices. Placing her gently on a splintery wooden floor. Rising above and fucking her, jamming myself into her until all she can do is make little grunts with each thrust. She spits at me, "You can't do it! You can't make me come."

The hatred ages her, contorting the fragile feminine beauty into something hard and mean. I wish I could do the same. The thought excites me, and suddenly I withdraw from her, shooting all over her, the first jets soaking into her sandy hair, the others dribbling down until a pool of it stands, stagnant, in her sparse pubic hair. Time will tell if I'm successful in this half-assed effort at protectiveness. Will she one day turn up in some health clinic, tearful before a counselor who informs her of the dreaded news...a lifetime of protease inhibitors and dark thoughts, wondering how much of a future she has left?

Perhaps I'm already too late. Felicity's passion is born of much experience.

*

Later, after the effects of the Seven have worn off, replaced by a wicked crystal high, my penis shriveled to a tiny egg in a nest of pubic hair, I turn the tables. Joshua, a shaved, pierced, muscled, and tattooed bouncer from the Façade leads me into a darkened area, a kind of sun porch, where we whisper together, groping, smoking crystal through a straw from a little brown glass bottle, a bent piece of wire its stem, until our nerves are fairly singing with chemicals. My memory lapses. I go from kissing Joshua, sucking and biting his tongue, his lips, and feeling his muscled cranium crushing into my neck, tickling, hurting, making me want to scream. *Cut.* I find myself on a scarred oak table, the plants covering its surface shoved to the floor, broken clay pots and soil everywhere, getting ruthlessly fucked on my back. It is women I prefer, but when the drugs and the alcohol combine to increase desire while at the same time stealing the ability, a pretty boy does nicely. The circles I've traveled in...this is a lesson I learned early on. And Joshua is a pretty boy...a perfectly shaped head, a cleft in his chin, stubble framing full lips, eyes so dark one could drown in them. He pounds into me, whispering over and over, "You're beautiful," as I try to get down inside myself and actually feel something.

Pain would be welcome. But there is nothing, save for an unwelcome fullness that reminds me of needing to have a bowel movement. I have become Felicity from earlier in the evening, wanting to be fucked so hard it will rouse some kind of emotion within me, some dim vestige of pleasure. But no one can fuck me that hard. Toward the end, though, there is some reward, a rush of blood that stains Joshua's pubic hair, a smear of crimson across his dripping cock. I suppose watching the anxious embarrassment cross his handsome features does filter through the emptiness.

"I'm sorry," I whisper, sitting upright on the table.

He grins, as if pleased with himself, staring down at his drooping cock, a drop of come poised at its tip. "It's cool. I did you right."

"Yeah," I mumble, feeling the heat of the blood and his come trickling from inside me. "Fucked me until I bled. Go brag about it."

As I head away from him, I hear him calling, "C'mon, man, I didn't mean it that way."

Who really cares what he meant?

It's at that point I decide to clean up and head for home.

*

And now I find myself a wraith, haunting the night-slicked streets of Chicago's Near North Side, thinking of London, walking through the foggy streets of Westminster on another night, with the same kind of evening behind me. I just want to get home, pop a few Xanax, and lie down, letting sleep draw a curtain across the day. Tomorrow will be my birthday; the sun will rise. Perhaps Henrietta will call and we'll go out for dinner, two old friends, except now we look like mother and son, and Henrietta hates that.

A figure passes. I keep my eyes averted, concentrating on the distended pattern of light on the wet pavement.

A stranger stops behind me. I sense his stillness. *Oh God, not tonight*, I think. My looks have been a curse... Everyone wants to take a ride on the Gary Adrion glory train, even strangers in the street. *Just leave me alone. Let me get home, crawl into my shell.*

I cast a quick look out of the corner of my eye and see a man's figure, long dark coat, valise in one hand. I wonder for just an instant, imagination spurred on by drugs, quiet, and fog, if this is a representative from hell, come to spirit me away. At this point it wouldn't matter much.

Stop that now. I move again, pace quickening. Not far to my front door.

But apparently not far enough. A voice calls out, "Gary? Is that you?"

I bite my lip, thinking of ignoring the cry, the half-familiar voice. I want so much to get home, to black out. I'm not ready to talk to anyone. I tentatively step forward but know, deep down, to whom the voice belongs. Sighing, I turn around, play out the ruse.

"Yes, it's me." The consummate actor, I peer through the fog and the darkness, even though by now I'm certain with whom I share the street.

He moves closer, face revealed in a flicker by the sodium vapor light. And what a face! I haven't seen him in years, and time has not been kind. His hair, close-cropped, reveals a shiny dome of flesh. Oval glasses cling to the bridge of his nose, but they don't hide the network of tiny cracks and broken veins surrounding his bright blue eyes. Jowls hang at his white collar. A topography of time spreads across his forehead and around his mouth. I let none of these observations show. Instead I smile. "Why, it's Liam Howard! What brings you out so late?"

I can see from the softening of his features and the smile that lights up his face, crinkling the withered flesh around his eyes, that he is pleased with my recognition. It has been years since we've seen each other.

"Actually," he says, "I was coming to see you." He laughs, a bit self-consciously, but for Liam, that's normal. Over the years his face may have changed, but he hasn't relaxed much. And yet I suddenly find myself missing his proper demeanor, his earnestness.

"Oh?"

"Well, of course, not this late. I had been by earlier, and when you weren't in, I went to Starbucks, had a cup of coffee. I just went back and tried you again. I'm glad I didn't miss you completely."

I rub the stubble on my chin. "Why didn't you call, Liam? We could have set something up."

"Oh, you know how it is. One gets busy..." his voice trails off.

I laugh. "But why the urgency? You could have called tomorrow morning." I'm puzzled. This is unlike the Liam I thought I knew. One thing I could always rely on was the fact that Liam was anything but impulsive.

"I'm moving to New York," he says. "I've been fortunate enough to get a show at the Guggenheim. It just seems that more is happening for me there than here, and I thought I'd give my luck a try in the Big Apple."

He smiles, self-conscious again. Liam is not one to brag. The Guggenheim? Impressive.

"I meant to see you. I even called several times, but you were never in. I didn't want to leave without saying goodbye."

"That's sweet." I stare down at the concrete sidewalk, shrouded in mist. My resolution to go home and crawl into bed is crumbling. "When are you leaving?"

"I have a red-eye flight out at 6:00 a.m."

"Well, then you must come over and have a drink. We'll toast to your future."

He looks relieved; the features relax for a moment. "I'd like that."

We walk the quiet streets back to my building. It has been a long time since I've been with Liam, and I wonder if what has transpired in that time has created a gulf between us, one that cannot be broached, no matter how much either of us wants to.

The lobby is brightly lit, brass, chrome, and marble glittering. I'm glad that Tom, the night doorman, is asleep at his post, chin resting on his chest. I wouldn't want to explain why I'm bringing an old man home in the middle of the night. There is enough talk about me already.

*

Once we are settled in my living room, a tumbler of Glenlivet on the rocks in each of our hands, the conversation dies. We've talked of where Liam will live, comparing New York to Chicago, how Liam's career has progressed.

It's getting very late, and we have fallen silent. It's dead quiet. After 2:00 a.m. I am just about to tell Liam that I'm very tired and need to get some sleep and that he probably should too, when he speaks once more.

"I didn't just come to say goodbye."

His face looks sheepish, making me wonder what's on its way. *Please don't tell me you want to lie down in bed with me just this once, that to hold me would be enough.* I've had the same story from characters who look just like Liam. Some have even offered to pay. As if I could be tempted by cash.

He stares down at the floor and then looks up. "To be perfectly honest, Gary, I've heard things about you, and it concerns me."

Oh no...

"I try to shrug things off, idle gossip, jealous tongues. But there have been too many reports, some of them from reliable sources, for me just to discount them."

I feel my scalp begin to prickle, heat rising to my face. Getting angry. I don't need this.

"I'm worried about you." His voice falters, and I think he can tell he's treading on dangerous ground. "I heard you're using heroin. I heard you're using Seven. Haven't you seen what each of those horrors have done to people? Heroin simply sucks away life. I've seen it time and time again in the art world. Promise and vitality snuffed out by an ugly beige powder that takes over. And Seven! Why did anyone have to invent such a hateful substance? You've heard, of course, about the delayed reaction...the facial paralysis that takes years to manifest itself...and then one day one wakes up with what looks like Bell's palsy! Gary, you can't let those things happen to you." Liam pauses, staring down into the amber liquid in his glass. "I've also heard you have a penchant for corruption. The father of a young girl I'd once photographed..."

"I don't need this, Liam," I say, my voice low but intense. "People talk. They will always talk. You and I haven't seen each other in a long time. You really have no idea of what my life is like." I light a cigarette. "Look, I've been playing the recreational drug game for years now." I lean forward and take his face in both my hands, forcing him to look at me when I play my trump card. "Liam...for all the abuse...do I look any worse for the wear?"

"No, no, of course you don't." He closes his eyes, opens them again. "I don't know how you do it. You haven't changed in twenty years." He shakes his head. "I don't think I want to know. But as far as not knowing what your life is like, I think I do." Softly. Firmly.

"No, I don't think you do! Damn it, Liam. What I do is my own business. I'll thank you to keep out of it."

"I wish I could," Liam says, the passion rising in his voice. "But I care about you. I always have, and I don't want to see you squander your life this way. Do you realize what you could do to yourself?"

"Of course I realize what I could do to myself. My head is above water at all times. Things are under control."

"You can stop anytime you like, right?"

His smugness fuels a low-burning spark of rage. "Don't be holier than thou, Liam. It doesn't become you."

"I'm not holier than anyone. I just don't want to see you this way. I've heard that there are certain places that will no longer admit you. That they're afraid of you. Now, I can't imagine anyone being afraid of you, but their fear does give me pause."

"Well, you have a brand-new life to go to now. I suggest you get to it and quit bothering me with your so-called concern for my life. I'm doing just fine. Can't you see that? Look at this face, this body. Do I look like I'm running myself down?"

"As I said, you look like the day I first met you."

I grow silent.

He comes back to the theme, a theme I now regret having ever brought up. "How can that be, Gary? Facelifts? Collagen? Liposuction? Body sculpting? I've seen people who look younger than their years, but no one can hold a candle to you in that department."

I almost blurt out that he is responsible for my alleged good fortune. If it hadn't been for him and his damn holograms... "You're out of line here, Liam."

"I don't think so."

"I repeat, you don't know me."

"No, I don't. To really know you, I'd have to see your soul, and since I can't, maybe I should be on my way. God knows that whatever you have showing to the rest of the world is not the real you." He begins gathering up his coat and valise. "I'll just be on my way, Gary. I'm sorry if I stirred up some hard feelings. I still love you, and I hope you can forget this."

Something he's said makes me stop. I bite my lower lip, feeling a curious mixture of hatred for him because he's brought up the things I try to escape on a daily basis, and for arousing in me the need to go to him as one might go to a parent, for solace and aid. "You know, Liam, if you'd like…" I pause for a minute, considering the momentousness of what I am about to say. "You can see my soul. If you really want to."

He doesn't look at me, facing the door. "No one can see your soul but God. Don't blaspheme. It may be trendy and 'cool' with your friends, but don't do it with me."

I lay a hand on his shoulder, feel him stiffen. "No, really, you can see it. Would you like to?"

"Stop it."

"Just let me prove it to you. It'll take only a few minutes of your time."

He turns, eyes bright with tears. "I don't know what you're up to. It makes me sad to see you like this. But whatever it is you want to show me, well, if you think it will help me understand this life you've chosen, then I guess I can spare you a few minutes."

"How gracious of you!" I cry, the sarcasm dripping. It will be interesting for the artist to see how his work has become organic, how it's grown over the years.

I will relish the stunned look of horror when I pull back my mother's old silk scarf.

"We need to go down to the basement, to my storage room. The story of my life, I guess you could say, is locked away there."

"What is it? Some kind of journal?"

I put a finger to his lips. "Shhh... You'll see."

Chapter Twenty

LIAM

Gary and I took the freight elevator down, down, deep into the bowels of this monolithic building he called home. The elevator made odd creaking sounds, light flashing as we passed different floors. We were quiet, the only sounds the cables above us whirring. Gary kept his eyes focused upward, watching the lights change for each floor. I could see a smile playing about his lips.

We exited the elevator. The basement's light was dim. Bare bulbs hung, irregularly spaced. Their glow fell in pools on the concrete floor. As we passed through the shadows, fingers of dread took hold...as if someone or something could be lying in wait where the light did not penetrate.

I suddenly wasn't so sure this was a good idea. I flashed on that hot August day when I first saw Gary, electrified by the charms of his beauty, on the L train. I remembered, though, the fear when I impulsively followed him, and we found ourselves alone in an alley. The chill that ran up my spine in spite of the heat. The fear that he might do me harm. A presentiment?

I felt that way now as I once more followed him into a situation that had an unpredictable outcome.

Everything comes full circle.

Gary paused before a padlocked door. "Are you ready?"

"Ready for what?" My words were thick. I was already wondering if he'd think me too strange if I just walked out, went back upstairs, got my things, and left. Reason told me that's just what I should be doing.

But that would be too impulsive for the likes of Liam Howard. I wouldn't want to appear a fool.

"You'll see," Gary said, grinning. He fitted a key into the padlock and opened the door. A rush of cool air emerged, bearing on it the odors of mildew and must. Dust. I sneezed.

I looked down at my watch. "I hope this won't take long. I need to be thinking about getting out to O'Hare."

Gary smiled. "There are cabs going by my building every five minutes, even now. You have nothing to worry about. Come on in."

Gary entered the room, switched on a buzzing fluorescent light.

At first I couldn't see what on earth had made me so unreasonably afraid. The storage room was typical—odd pieces of furniture, stacked boxes, and shelves covered with a mixture of belongings that probably should have been discarded. A long table fronted the shelves. On it were some stacks of books, an old mallet, and a large round object, shrouded in purple silk, leaning against the wall.

Gary looked at me then, not just a glance but something more in-depth, as if he were trying to see inside me. As if he were looking at me for the last time...

Don't be ridiculous.

He said no more but went over to the purple-shrouded object and slowly drew away the silk.

Before I even saw it, I knew what it was. My hologram of him, created all those years ago. He paused in unveiling the thing to bend over and plug in the cord that would bring to life the tiny Gary I had created. A queasy mixture of dread and desire set my heart to pounding, sweat popping up in beads on my forehead. There was something about this suspenseful presentation that led me to think I would be seeing more than an example of my work some seventeen years ago.

I bit my lip as he revealed more and more. As he drew away the fabric, I didn't believe what I was seeing. And when finally the thing was revealed to me fully, I gasped and stumbled backward.

"What is this? Some kind of joke?" I tried to appear as if I too were in on the sick humor. "What did you do?"

"Only through the touch of God," Gary whispered. "Or maybe the devil."

"I don't understand." My words trailed off. The room was spinning. I felt sick. The hologram, or what it had essentially been, remained. The form of Gary was the same. I drew closer, with the same dread one might approach an auto accident or a crime scene. Gary's skin had aged...sagging jowls, thinning hair, crow's-feet around the eyes, deepening laugh lines encircling the lips, which had seemed to grow thinner, crueler. Across his forehead, a network of horizontal lines. I remembered the perfect body that had once graced this portrait. That body had vanished, leaving in its wake a thin, emaciated wraith, rib and pelvic bones poking out from beneath sagging muscles.

All of these things were terrible, and I gasped "It can't be," not wanting to fully integrate the truth. My hologram of Gary had aged while he had not.

But the signs of aging were not the true horror of the portrait. No, those lay in the needle tracks running up and down his arms, the glazed eyes, filmed over, with their network of broken blood vessels, and worst of all, the small, dark lesions that covered skin that had once been so smooth and perfect as to appear luminescent.

And the face! That beautiful face, so perfect as to appear unreal, carved by a sculptor. As I moved around the dome, I saw the real horror. Bad enough that one side of it had aged, marred by wrinkles, KS lesions, and a network of bursting blood vessels. But when I saw the other side of his face, with all the carnage I've already mentioned—I sucked in some air as I saw that side of the face had sagged, the lips drooping. His face was monstrous...a through-the-windshield car accident that had occurred, it seemed, when the driver had a horrible stroke.

One word sprang to mind, one hateful word.

Seven.

I began to cry, mumbling, "Tell me this is a joke."

"This is my soul," Gary said.

"This is the devil."

"We all have heaven and hell inside each of us. Except with me, the hell stays in the hologram, and the heaven stays on my face."

I said nothing, staring. My stomach churned.

Finally, "Perhaps if we pray together, Gary..." I reached out to touch his shoulder, and he moved angrily away, jerking himself out of my reach. "Gary, we have to pray. This isn't right. It's not too late!"

His back was turned.

"What are you doing?" My voice rose, hysterical. "What are you doing?" I screamed. I already knew what he would have in his hands when he turned, but I was too logical to believe it. Crime never happens to people like me.

But I had seen too much.

Gary turned around, a smile playing about his perfect face. It belied the mallet he held aloft in one hand.

I put up a hand in defense, backing as he approached. Even as the words spilled, gasping, from my lips, I knew they were not true. "It's not too late."

Chapter Twenty-One

GARY

There is blood on my hands. I look down at a body, a body that's become a thing—monstrous, ugly, inanimate. It could be a sculpture, a figure formed from wax or porcelain. The soul inside is gone, leaving a shell. I wipe a thin line of sweat from my forehead with a trembling hand, trying to tell myself these things, trying to believe that what lies at my feet is nothing more than an object, something to be reviled, something not worthy of further consideration.

It's not easy to believe what I am trying to tell myself. Although the corpse does not have a twinkle in its eye or the simple rise and fall of a chest, it's hard to remove myself from the plain fact that the body possessed those movements, those simple signs of life, just minutes ago. Distance, for now, seems more a matter of location than of feeling. The body at my feet wears the badges of its untimely demise—a dented face, a split-open skull, blood and grayish-pink brain matter seeping out.

I stoop, plunge my fingers into the deepest hole, the one on the belly, to feel the warmth and the entrails. Amazed that the breathing has stopped. Amazed that I have such power.

I lift a finger to my mouth and slowly run it over my lips, the blackish liquid warm and viscous, metallic to the taste. I recall the vampire films I loved as a youth, never really believing such a thing could exist.

Now I do.

I have stolen a life so that my own might continue. There is something vampiric in that, isn't there? Because without this theft of a beating heart and an expanding and contracting pair of lungs, I would be unable to live myself.

Isn't that the real essence of the vampire?

It seems too quiet here. A dull clanging is my only accompaniment, pipes bringing warmth and water to scores of tenants above, whose lives continue, ignorant, untouched by my murderous hand. And that's the amazing thing, the thing that causes my breath, when drawn inward, to quiver.

Life goes on, in spite of this monumental act, just a quick, surprised scream and a heartbeat away.

There is blood on the walls, spattered Jackson Pollock-style. Who can say what is art and what is murder?

Liam, my friend, my admirer, the man who once recorded my beauty in the medium of holography, now lies in final repose on a cold concrete floor, staring vacantly at nothing or perhaps at the hell that will one day consume me. He can no longer chastise me, can no longer beg me to drop to my knees with him and pray, pray for forgiveness, imploring Jesus to lead me down the path of the righteous.

It's not too late, he said before I brought the mallet down on his head, his throat, his gut, an eye socket, his back as he fell, anywhere the mallet would wound, destroy, suck...life.

Liam was wrong. The final irony of his existence, I suppose, is that he thought he had the power to do anything, to change another person, whom, I must admit, he cared very deeply about.

I turn, looking at the mess in the room, glad I fortified myself earlier with cocaine and crystal. There is much work to be done here.

I suddenly stop and scream, lowering my head into my hands. I dissolve into sobs, muttering, "Oh God, what have I done? What have I done?"

I try to distance myself, try to rationalize. *What business did he have coming here? Who was he to tell me to pray? Where does he get off trying to push repentance on me? He's the one who caused everything...him and his lust for young men...a lust he never had the honesty to acknowledge.*

But it does no good. I cannot escape the fact that I am a killer. Some have already given me that dark, violent name, but those deaths, while attributable to me, certainly, were never by my own hand.

So this is what I've become. Murderer. I take in a few quivering breaths, calming myself, knowing that when the morning light rises above Lake Michigan, I will have to deal with this new facet of my personality. Will have to deal with the evidence, with evasion, with secrecy. I laugh... I've had years of practice for this new role.

Movement and action are the only solace I can have right now.

I take the freight elevator back upstairs. My apartment is as it was. I had expected there to be some magical transformation, some sign that I was now entering the lair of a killer. Life's accouterments can be so boring.

I go to the bar, pour myself a quick shot of scotch, down it, and rub my hands, wondering where to begin. I see Liam's things lying on an armchair near the window, his coat and valise. The sight, for just a second, seems unbearably poignant, and I catch my breath. Then I gather them up, take them into the kitchen, where I stuff them into a black Hefty bag. Later I will weigh the bag down and drop it into the lake.

There must be no record of his visit here tonight. Because of the trip Liam was making and because of his extremely limited circle of close friends, it will be days, perhaps weeks, before an alarm is raised and he is reported missing. That cold trail can only be my ally.

I bite my lip, wishing I could stop the emotional roller coaster I've boarded. The hot tears sting, the shame makes me physically ill, and I realize *I cannot afford these luxuries.*

There is work to be done. An alibi to be concocted, just in case...

After slipping into a long cashmere overcoat, I take the freight elevator back downstairs to the first floor. I pull back the grate and slip quickly out the service entrance. The sky is lightening. No sun yet, but that peculiar blue-gray shade that characterizes predawn, that gives form and ever-increasing definition to the world.

I close my eyes, breathing in the cold air to clear my head, to prepare myself for the small but crucial role I am about to play.

I hurry around to the front of the building, grateful for the fact that our doorman is more of a dormouse. I'm sure he didn't see Liam and me enter the building earlier.

I approach the door, and there's Tom, his broken-veined, middle-aged Irish face lit up, waving. I glide through the revolving doors and smile. Even though he's smiling, there is wariness in his eyes, a look that says *What's this one been up to now?*

"Hello, Tom!" I call.

"Late night, Mr. Adrion?"

"Yes, it's my birthday, and I've been out celebrating."

"There was a friend of yours here earlier tonight." Tom consults something on his console. "A Mr. Howard."

"Really? Did he leave a message?"

"He said he'd be back. Good thing, I guess, that he gave up on you."

I smile. "Yes, a good thing for him... Wouldn't get much sleep waiting around for me." I flash on a macabre scene, just beneath us, of the eternally resting Liam lying ruined in my basement. For a moment I fear I might lose consciousness. The room spins. I falter and stumble.

Tom laughs. "You okay, Mr. Adrion?"

I breathe in deeply, gripping the wall for support. "A little too much celebration."

I stop at the door, grope in my pockets. Tom is a lazy bastard, and tonight it will serve me well. I'm glad I can rely on the fact that he would wait for me to open the door myself rather than lifting a finger to buzz me in. I sigh, disgusted, and turn to him. "Forgot my keys... Wouldn't you know it?"

"I'll buzz you right in, Mr. Adrion."

"That's fine, Tom, but I'm going to need the master to get into my apartment."

"Right." He digs in the cubbyholes behind him for a key I don't need. I cross to the desk and take it from him. "Thank you, Tom. I'll bring this right back."

"Take your time, Mr. Adrion."

I ride up in the elevator, congratulating myself on a *memorable* performance. It's miserable that I have to think this way, though. But understand, this is all I have to cling to now, this new secret, this new struggle for survival, which is all my life has been anyway. Some might say "Ah, let's feel sorry for poor Gary Adrion. He's one of the handsomest men most people will ever see, and not only that, he doesn't age!"

What those people don't realize is that the drugs, the alcohol, the sex are only escapes from this web I've entangled myself in. How am I to ever love anyone when I have this awful secret, now multiplied by two, in my basement? Love is what we all long for in the end, and I'm uncertain I can ever have it. So to those people who think I'm blessed, I say *fuck you*.

I come back to the apartment once more, never having been in and out of it so many times in such a short period. My head buzzes with the lingering effects of the drugs and the extreme tension of just having killed one of the few people in this world who did love me. I collapse onto the couch, too fatigued, in spite of the stimulants racing through my bloodstream, to cry.

I go to the medicine cabinet, take out the Xanax, wash it down with the dregs of scotch remaining in my crystal tumbler, and go to my bedroom, where I strip off my bloody clothes—these too will have to be sunk in Lake Michigan—and fall onto my bed, willing sleep to come, to escape once more.

*

When I awaken, I realize there is still much to be done. A body lies in my basement, a huge pointing finger that will not go away on its own.

The idea of food sickens me, and I sit and stare out the window at a gray day. The traffic streaming by on Lake Shore Drive below reminds me there are scores of people out there who lead normal lives. They're off to work, kiss the wife and kiddies goodbye, come home in the evening to dinner and TV.

I think about the problem of the body, and it isn't long before I come to a solution. I find my leather-bound address book and look up a number for an old friend. Someone who has since turned his back on me. I must go to Andy Crause, even if he once swore that I should never darken his doorstep again. Desperation takes away one's pride.

The number is there... Andy Crause, University of Chicago. A chemistry professor...someone who works with acids, who knows what it takes to work the alchemy that will make a body disappear. I nod. He will be very surprised to hear from me.

An hour later my phone rings. I lift it.

Tom. "There's a Mr. Crause here to see you, sir."

"Send him right up. Thanks."

Andy Crause has aged since I last saw him. Once a handsome youth, a doctoral candidate in chemistry, the two of us had enjoyed together what Chicago's darker, late-night side has to offer. I must admit I pushed the guy into plumbing new depths of depravity, not that he wasn't a willing student. But his Irish Catholic guilt finally made him push me away. Sometimes one has to push Gary Adrion away if one is to survive.

As soon as I open the door, I meet his dour expression, the dullness in his brown eyes as he stares listlessly. He doesn't want to be here; that much is plain. There is no hiding it behind the small oval-framed stainless steel glasses. His florid Irish skin has begun to sag, and his waist is thickening, marring what was once a spectacularly muscled body.

"Andy!" I cry, turning on the jovial voice and the smile as other people would flip a light switch. "Good to see you. It's been a long time."

"What do you want, Gary?"

"What do I want? My, aren't we direct this morning?"

"Cut it. This isn't a social call. You said something about a matter of life and death. I wouldn't be here otherwise. I thought you understood that I finished with you back when..." He pauses. "Never mind."

I feel stupid standing there smiling at him. There's no need for the ruse. I step back. "Won't you come in?"

He walks by without looking at me. He doesn't look over my place, doesn't stop, heads instead for a chair, which he plops down in with resignation. "What do you want?"

"I need your help."

He nods. "You already said that. And I already said I didn't think there would be anything I could possibly be willing to help *you* with."

"I've gotten myself into a bit of a jam."

He snorts a brief, mirthless laugh. "Why doesn't that surprise me?"

"No, you don't understand. This is serious."

"It always is for self-absorbed people like you."

Normally I wouldn't let a dig like that pass unchallenged, but my situation calls for desperate measures. "I know what you're thinking."

"You couldn't possibly. You don't even know me. You knew me once, but that person is gone. Forever, I hope. Did you know I've gotten tenure? Did you know I got married? Did you know I have a daughter...all of three years old? There's nothing you could possibly want to do with me that I'd be interested in."

"Then why are you here?"

"I don't know." He gets up and starts to head for the door. I rush over to stand in front of him.

"Please. You've come this far. At least hear me out."

He rolls his eyes, adopts a sullen, droop-shouldered pose. He does not sit down again. "Go ahead."

I close my eyes, deciding to be direct. "Someone has died because of me, Andy. I didn't want it to happen, but somehow it did."

"I'm still not surprised, and if you think I want to get involved with something like this, you're even crazier than I thought."

I place my hands on his shoulders and can feel how he recoils at my touch. "Listen, I killed him. It was Liam Howard. You remember him?"

"Yes, and I'm sorry to hear this. I don't think I want to hear any more." He struggles from my grip and heads for the door again. He has turned pale.

I grab him, my hand connecting with the wool of his jacket. He yells at me, "I don't want to hear any more, Gary! I should never have come here."

"I could go to prison for this, Andy. For life!"

"Send me a postcard."

"Stop being so flippant." My breath is coming faster, and I'm getting afraid the problem of disposing of Liam's body will be mine alone. I can't bear the thought of seeing him again, seeing what I've done.

I pause, letting my heart slow, my breathing return to normal. Then I lean over and whisper something in his ear. A memory, if you will.

"You're despicable."

"Would you like your fellow faculty members to know this about you? Would you like your lovely wife to see a whole new side of you?"

"You're blackmailing me."

"I'm sorry, Andy. Just help me this once."

"I don't see that I have much choice, you bastard."

I explain to him then what needs to be done, how the body must be destroyed. And how I know he will have the knowledge to do just that...irrevocably.

He shakes his head, giving me a sorrowful look with those dark brown eyes. "How dare you involve me in something like this," he says softly.

"I have no choice. Can you do it now...please?"

"I have no choice either." Now he won't even look at me. "I need some things," he says to the floor. "I have to go back to the lab."

"There's a phone on the desk over there. Call someone and have them bring it. You're not leaving until the job is done."

He shakes his head and moves toward the phone.

What have I become?

*

A young man, dressed in baggy jeans and a sweatshirt, arrives after about a half hour, laden down with a cardboard box, clinking of glass inside.

"Just set it on the floor, Tim. I really appreciate it." Andy takes out his wallet.

Tim holds up his hand. "There's no need for that."

"Take it. Cab fare, at least."

The boy pockets the money and is gone.

I pick up the box. "Let's go."

*

Downstairs, I set the box on the floor and fish my keys out. When I open the door, a wave of air rushes out of the room, and the decay is already beginning to manifest itself. Andy peers over my shoulder.

"God!"

"I *am* really sorry you have to see this. I wish it could be any other way. But you're the only one who can help me."

Liam is where I left him, on his back on the floor. The wounds have dried on his body. The blood is almost black, crusty. One eye dangles on his cheek, and the other stares upward—at Heaven, I hope—already bearing a milky film.

I push Andy into the room. I need to be strong. Otherwise I'll start screaming, and I don't know when I'll stop.

"How long will it take?"

"A few hours." Andy crouches beside the body and shudders. A spasm of snotty breath escapes him. He turns to me. "Get out."

I say nothing, just turn and close the door slowly, until it clicks.

*

Later, the phone rings.

"Hello."

It's the doorman. "A Mr. Crause, sir, just left. He said to let you know."

"Thanks." I put the phone down, weary. I go to the window, stare outside at the golden light of the dying afternoon. Then I go downstairs.

When I open the door, the room is clean, save for the acrid odor of nitric acid.

Just before I switch off the lights, I see the hologram, still uncovered. I wonder what Andy Crause thought of it, wonder if he even recognized who it was. I go to throw the purple silk over it and pause, my hand to my mouth.

There is a splash of color now... Crimson drips from the hands.

Chapter Twenty-Two

HENRIETTA

The party was in full swing. And I was too, looking damn good for a gal my age. Oh Lord, how could I still say something like that and hold my head up? But the mirror didn't lie. Foundation could only hide so much. The battle with the big old crows who came and walked around near my eyes at night was not an optimistic one. The crows were winning. But still, in my Armani dress, a red wig, and satin pumps, I could still catch the eye of an unwary man.

I sat in a corner of the room, a gallery space on West Superior...Timothy Bright, Ltd. The show was a benefit for Absolutely Positive, a support group for HIV-positive people in Chicago. I'd seen so many gals come and go down at the Façade that I feel it's important to do my part, and what's a hundred bucks for a party with free drinks and lots of gorgeous men to gape at?

The door opened, and so did my mouth. There, in all his glory, was Mr. Gary Adrion, looking just like the day I met him. He was wearing a pair of baggy gray slacks, a black suede vest, and a white collarless shirt. His hair, grown longer, was combed away from his face. He looked like something off the cover of *GQ*. And it made me angry. Who was he that he should be so blessed? What bargain had he made with the devil? Who was his plastic surgeon?

Someone the Jackson family was hooked up with, no doubt. I hadn't seen Gary in a while, what with his gallivanting off to Europe every six months or so and his whirlwind of a social life. And that was another thing. The rumors I'd heard of his party behavior should show up on that perfect face. You didn't act like an animal without growing a little fur. But Mr. Gary was in the pink, oh yes. Looked like he never touched a drop of alcohol or puffed on a cigarette, let alone that alphabet soup of chemicals that was all the rage.

I hurried over to the bar and freshened my drink, then sauntered over to our Mr. Adrion.

He switched to the eyes-lighting-up mode when he saw me. He had the smile down perfect, as well as the look of delight. But he couldn't quite get the eyes; they were dead.

"Henrietta! Good God, how long has it been?"

He pressed me to his chest, and I swear on a stack of Bibles I could feel the muscles rippling beneath his clothes. Made an old gal like me moist.

"Too long, honey. Why haven't you come and seen me?"

He shook his head and looked elsewhere, sorry, I bet, that he opened this can of worms. He opened his mouth, and I put a finger to it to silence him.

"You say one word about how busy you've been and I'll slap your face. I deserve better than that."

"Touché. I guess all I can do is offer up my humble apologies."

"There's nothing humble about someone who looks like you. Where have you been?"

"Here...there. I've been around."

"The circuit-party scene?"

"Well, some of that." He grinned, letting the boy show through. How a man of thirty-eight could let a bit of boy show through was a magic trick I'd love to learn.

"You don't need to waste your guilt on me, Gary. It's an emotion I discarded long ago. Worthless. Especially when one is in the pursuit of pleasure. And from what I hear, you've gone to great lengths to secure that."

"You shouldn't listen to idle gossip, Henrietta. You never know what is and isn't true."

"I only listen to the sources I can rely on. Enough about that. I asked you a question. Where have you been?"

"I was in London for a while, but I had to get back. I missed home."

"And I'm sure it missed you, honey. Seen Liam?"

That was when a funny thing happened. At the mention of Liam, all the color drained from Gary's face. I swear he looked like he was going to be sick. "Honey? You okay?"

"Yes! Yes, of course." He cast his gaze about the room. "Well, actually I'm not feeling a hundred percent tonight."

"You were out celebrating last night, I heard."

"Yes...that's it. A few too many party favors."

"Mm-hmm. I talked to Liam yesterday afternoon. I urged him to come and see you before he was off to New York. You know about that?"

"I'd heard from someone. I can't remember who, that he has a show there."

"Not just a show...the Guggenheim is exhibiting his stuff. He's become a great American genius. Unfortunately that equates to lowest-common-denominator pap. Ansel Adams instead of Diane Arbus."

Gary kept looking around the room. I knew the look... It was *Let me find someone to get me out of this* desperation. I wasn't letting him off the hook that easily, though. "So...did he manage to hook up with you or what?"

Gary shook his head. "No, I guess I got home too late."

"But he said he was determined to see you. Said he'd wait around until you got home if need be." I touched Gary's cheek. "He's been hearing some of the same shit as me, and he was concerned."

"Well, I didn't see him!"

The agitation, I thought, was uncalled for.

"You don't sound so innocent. What happened?"

"What are you talking about?" he snapped.

"Gary, I've known you for too long. You can't lie to me. You're far too keyed up for someone who's telling the truth." I knew what Liam could be like, and I also knew he had a little lecture in store for our boy. No one likes "little lectures," especially when they contain kernels of truth. I could imagine the scene. I could imagine the righteously indignant none-of-your-business reaction Gary would have given Liam. We are always most indignant when someone swings too close to the truth.

"Well, what you think and what I know are two different things."

"Did Liam lecture you?"

"I told you I didn't see him. Now, can we turn the page?"

I grinned. "No, honey, I don't think we can. Own up to it. Did you have a little spat with Liam on the eve of his departure?"

"You're insane."

I nodded. The anger was beginning to grow. I didn't have to take this shit. "We used to be able to talk to one another."

"Yes, but you yourself said people who dwell on the past are boring."

"And people who lie are even duller, especially when their lies are so fucking colorless." I started to walk away. "I'll be around when you have something at least mildly interesting to say."

And I walked away from him. Later, not much, I saw him hurrying out of the party, without a goodbye for anyone...even me.

Chapter Twenty-Three

GARY

A cold wind screams across the lake. Its waters are gray, roiling, throwing themselves with impotent fury against the boulders to my north, splashing up in a spray along the edges of the concrete pier upon which I stand. I take a look behind me and see the twinkling lights of the high-rises, the line of orderly headlights on Lake Shore Drive, as the masses make their way homeward from the city. Rush hour...the term has never meant anything to me. Instead it conjures up in me the numbing, nerve-jangling good feelings of pure cocaine.

I'm standing alone on the pier, the twilight causing me to fade fast from view, I'm sure. Everyone else is sensible enough to be inside this evening, when winter is making one last hurrah before spring takes over its position in the seasonal hierarchy. The wind is bitter cold, flecked with needles of freezing rain from above, icy waters from the lake below. The clouds on the horizon promise snow.

In my hand is a black plastic garbage bag, containing Liam's valise, his black wool coat, and the clothing I wore on the night I...on the night I...last saw him.

I have worn no gloves this bitter night, and my hands are beginning to itch and ache from the cold. I'm tempted to take one last look into the bag and decide against it.

What will it gain me? Opening it will release only the smells of damp wool and congealing blood. A Pandora's box of ugly memories.

Fortunately Liam's valise was the old-fashioned kind, hard and heavy, unlike the lightweight nylon bags most everyone uses these days. I figure it will weigh the garbage bag down enough to let it sink to the sandy bottom of Lake Michigan, leaving no trace, never to surface again.

I walk out farther, until I'm at the end of the pier, where a beacon glows in the lavender light of dusk. There is a metal railing, discarded beer cans, fishing detritus left behind by men in happier times. I clutch the cold railing and hoist the bag over the edge, watching as it sails upward into the darkness for just an instant, then drops quickly to the black waters, to float on the foam-flecked surface before disappearing.

I stare for several minutes, trying to ignore my shivering, waiting for the bag to bob back up, accusing.

But it doesn't. And after a while I turn back, shoving my hands into my pockets.

I thought this deed would be liberating. I had expected to feel a surge of relief. But it's as if my spirits are being dragged down into dark water with the last of Liam's possessions.

I hurry now across the hard-packed sand. A tunnel is up ahead, and once through it, I will climb a set of stairs and be on Lake Shore Drive. I can hail a taxi easily there, and this taxi will take me somewhere where I can chase away the demons that have been haunting me. Chase them away completely. Oblivion has its price. Luckily for me, that price can be counted in dollars.

I quicken my pace to cross the street, feeling exposed in the four lanes of waiting headlights and idling engines.

I can almost feel the eyes on me, accusing, as if they all know from what mission I've come.

Finally I am to the other side of the drive and can scan the cars for a yellow cab. I am where I need to be to go south...to a club where many of my circuit-party, arsty-crowd friends would be surprised to find me.

When at last a cab pulls up, engine chugging, I climb inside and give the driver the address. He turns. "Rough neighborhood, pal. I ain't supposed to say this, but I don't go down there."

I'm bored with him. I throw a fifty-dollar bill onto the front seat. "Now do you go there?"

The driver, a dark-skinned, Middle-Eastern looking sort, shifts the cab into gear and merges back into traffic.

*

The streets here on the south side of the city are dwarfed by the housing projects rising up all around us. Big square blocks of brick and cement, depressing.

"You sure you want to get out here?" The driver looks around at the empty streets, trash skittering along the sidewalks, the caged façades staring at us like empty eye sockets.

"I told you the address, didn't I?" I throw another fifty on the seat. "Now lock your doors and hightail it out of here."

The place is two doors up from where the taxi sits, idling. As soon as I slam the door shut, the cab is gone in a rush, trailing a line of blue-gray exhaust in its wake.

Once upon a time, this would have been the province of crack cocaine...a crack house but not a home. Now Seven has taken the place of those other chemical lifesavers. Seven, with its lovely adrenaline rush, its promise of aphrodisia...a promise that never fails to deliver. What person, especially a man, could resist its seductive allure?

No matter how dark the consequences.

And those of us who enjoy Seven's pleasures like to be together, to share the bounty, so to speak. This place is a little club, really, serving watered-down beer, with illegal slot machines in the front, couches and dark, stained carpeting in the back. One needs to have a membership for entry. Desperation and being in the know are the prices one pays for membership. If they don't know you behind the bar, you don't get in.

I am buzzed in without hesitation. Once inside, the place has the smell of old cigarette smoke and stale beer. I feel at home here. The bartender, a young black woman, says nothing when I order a beer. She pours from a pitcher; the beer is lukewarm and flat. No matter.

I take my beer and head through a curtained doorway to the back. I reach into the pockets of my trench coat, making sure the little bottle of pink tablets is there...oblivion in the form of a small disc.

In the back, bodies are strewn, heads lolling on chests. A woman with bright fuchsia hair sits close to a dark-skinned man, Indian perhaps, rubbing his chest and staring dully into his red-veined eyes. I find an empty sofa near the back, twist the lid off the bottle, and down two Sevens with beer.

The great thing, though, about Seven, is how well it works with heroin, reducing, if not removing, the initial nausea, while upping the ante on the mellow high, turning it into a rush not unlike orgasm.

I roll up my shirtsleeve and take a length of rubber from my pocket, wrap it tightly around my upper arm so the skin beneath bulges. I flick at the purple veins on my arm until I can feel one jutting above the surface of my smooth, unblemished skin. I rub it for a moment, thinking how this vein is an ally in my desire to leave the world behind. I pull out a small baggie, empty a little white powder into a bent-handled spoon, and then cook it with a disposable lighter until it melts and bubbles...a magical transformation. The syringe hungrily sucks up the liquid. Expertly, I squirt a little of the liquid out, making sure there is no air left inside the plastic. I find the bulging vein once more and, with a sigh, plunge the needle in. It hurts for just an instant, and then I pull it out. A drop of crimson beads up on my arm when I remove the rubber. I leave my shirtsleeve rolled up—after all, Egyptian cotton does not come cheap—and lean back against the grimy wall, close my eyes, and wait.

A voice, husky, raspy, causes me to open my eyes. "Good shit, Gary?"

I look up as a waifish woman kneels. Her hair, dirty blonde, stands up in stiff little spikes. Her breath is bad, and I can see why—the yellowed, rotting teeth. Yet this woman looks familiar, and it all comes back in a rush. Lucinda. I remember a party in Wicker Park so many years ago. Henrietta and I went there when I was still innocent. Lucinda had helped corrupt me. Cocaine and sex with a man who looked like a girl.

"You remember me?"

"Sure." I close my eyes again, willing her away.

"Got anything to share?"

Annoyed, I open my eyes again. The heroin and the Seven are beginning to kick in, making me feel slightly nauseated, while at the same time wrapping my brain in cotton swathing. I reach inside my pocket and take out the baggie. I hand it to her. "Now get out of here."

I close my eyes once more and listen as she skitters away, like a rat, across the rough hardwood of the scarred floor.

But she has ruined it for me. The drugs no longer seem to work. In spite of the rushing of my heart and the erection that lazes in my pants, they have done nothing to reduce my despair. That particular emotion still hangs over me, like a cold, wet cloak. Henrietta once said, "To cure the soul by means of the senses and the senses by means of the soul." It no longer works. I could probably fuck Lucinda once more, bury myself deep within her diseased ass and not worry about the consequences, but I know this would only make me feel worse.

Lucinda has probably lived a life no more debauched than my own. Yet she has had to pay the price. Even in the dim half-light of this back room, it's obvious her skin is sallow, eyes reddened and sore, and hair thin and dirty. Yet I do the same thing and never once undercut the bloom of good health...of being in the pink, if you will.

It isn't fair, and I'm sick of it. The room tilts a little as I get to my feet. I should just go home now. Home and begin anew.

I walk to the front of the bar, where Lucinda's head droops over a glass of beer. A cigarette has burned down to the filter between her grimy fingers.

A few other people share the bar with her, dark, bundled souls who no longer even attempt to make conversation, but who sit hunched over, heads drooping like dying flowers over glasses of tepid flat beer.

I open the door, and the cold rushes in to touch my heated face with icy fingers. Winter is having a last hurrah. The sky rains down a light, fluffy snow.

"See you around, Prince Charming."

I stiffen at the sound of Lucinda's voice. It has been so many years since anyone has called me that. And all at once, it triggers the memory of the beautiful young girl who once christened me with the name. It almost seems as if that history happened to someone else.

I do not turn and look back. I button my coat, turn the collar up, and head out into the wind.

But I don't walk far. I lean against a building, hand shielding my eyes from the snow, and weep. The sobs come from nowhere, sudden, without warning. What have I done to myself? I had once envisioned a life in which I would be a husband and father, the Currier and Ives ideal of the American family. Kiddies gathered 'round in front of a roaring fire while I read to them from a big book of illustrated Hans Christian Andersen fairy tales and Mama looked on. And I know now that's not ever to be. If I had married when I was younger, my wife would now show the signs of age, graying hair and wrinkling skin, while I still retained the bloom and health of a boy. She would resent me for it. What woman wouldn't? And she would hate me. Eventually my children would surpass me in the physical manifestations of age, and how would I explain that?

I have sought out all the earthly pleasures...sex, drugs, fine things...and not one of them has given me any succor, has made my life any more enriched.

I wipe angrily at my eyes. I need to be getting home. Perhaps...perhaps it's not too late. Perhaps if I turn things around and leave the evil behind, I can be Prince Charming once more. Perhaps I can reverse what is in the hologram by doing only good.

Perhaps. I begin to hurry away. There are footfalls behind me, and I have no desire to see or communicate with anyone else.

Chapter Twenty-Four

DAVIO

I knew as soon as I heard her call out "Prince Charming" who he was. I had thought there was something familiar when I saw him come into the club, those fine clothes and the face that could stop traffic. Oh man, I just knew it! I'd waited a lifetime to run into this Prince Charming again. I remembered seeing him with Zoe, that sunny August day from another lifetime that now existed in some sort of movie. He had ridden by us on his bicycle in Lincoln Park. Zoe had been so excited, her face aglow. When the woman at the bar called him Prince Charming, I knew.

I guzzled the last dregs of my beer and stood, waiting for my equilibrium to balance so I could pursue the fucker who ruined my sister's life. Who, really, murdered her.

I had carried this hatred around for so many years that my heart had corroded, causing it to shrivel and blacken. Once I lost Zoe, there could be no pleasure, no happiness. The best I could ever hope for was the forgetting that came from getting fucked up, which I did on a regular basis. Whenever I had leave from the Army, I headed straight for the bars, the houses of prostitution, and now the places where Seven and a crack rock came cheap and easy.

It was cold outside. It hit me like a slap as I walked into it, pulling my fatigue jacket tighter. I could see the fucker ahead, leaning unsteadily against a wall. Prince Charming...right. I'll Prince Charming his ass right into hell.

I fingered the switchblade in my pocket. A man needed protection in this life, and this cold, sharp blade of stainless steel was mine. It had gotten me out of many a scrape in my day, but I always had it at the ready, waiting, waiting for the day when I knew I would have the opportunity to avenge my little sister.

He was walking away...fast. The cold night air helped clear my head, and I picked up my pace. I wished for more light. The night was cloud-covered, no moon, no stars. And here in this godforsaken part of town, half the streetlights weren't working...their light shot out by gangbangers, I guess.

"Hey!" I cried. "Hey, you! Slow down."

He stopped and stiffened. He turned to see if it was really he who was being accosted. *You bet your pretty ass it's you.*

I caught up to him, holding on to his sleeve while I caught my breath. He looked me over, trying, I suppose, to place where he knew me from or what I wanted from him.

"Yes?" He cocked his head.

I bit my lip so hard I could taste the copper of my blood, licked away at it. I was so furious I couldn't say anything. Finally, "Prince Charming...right?"

He gave me this sort of pathetic half smile. "What are you talking about?"

"The bitch at the bar back there, she called you Prince Charming."

"I don't know who you are or what you want...and I'd say the same for the young lady at the bar."

"Don't deny it." I grinned. "I been lookin' for Prince Charming all my life."

He closed his eyes, and I could see disgust emanating off him like an odor.

"I'm not into that scene."

What the fuck! I couldn't help myself, I belted him a good one across the face. It sent him reeling until he landed, with a big outrush of air, against a brick wall. He rubbed at his face, staring at me.

"What's with you?"

"You may think everybody wants that pretty face, Prince Charming, but I don't. I think it's pretty ugly myself, pretty ugly for what it done to my sister."

"I don't know what you mean. Calm down, man, and tell me what you think I did."

"Let me introduce myself, you cocksucker. I'm Davio D'Angelo. D'Angelo! Does that name ring a bell?"

I saw something cross his features, but I can't say for sure if it was fear or remembering.

"I'm sorry. I think you have me confused with someone else. I'll forget the slap. Just let me get on my way."

I could see him furiously scanning the street for a taxi, which reminded me. If I was going to do this, I didn't have much time. I took the switchblade from my pocket and clicked it open. "You killed my sister. And you know what, asshole? I swore to her I would kill whoever hurt her. Now you get yours." I made a lunge at him, the knife upraised, but he was able to skirt me, jumping out of the way with a litheness and grace I had long ago lost. He grabbed my arm.

"Wait! Just wait a minute!" He was breathing heavy now, and I knew he was scared. "Just who the hell do you think I am?"

"Oh, don't play that shit with me, man. I know you... I saw you once...and my sister called you Prince Charming. You're the fucker who made her kill herself."

I swiped at him with the knife, succeeding only in gashing his coat sleeve.

"Hold on, damn it! When? When did this happen? When did I supposedly do this to your sister?"

"I been nursin' this grudge for, like, seventeen years. And my hatred for you hasn't gotten one iota less. You're gonna pay."

"Will you listen to yourself? Seventeen years ago? That man would be middle-aged now."

He dragged me by my coat sleeve to where a streetlight still managed to give off its sodium vapor glow.

"Do I look like a middle-aged man to you?"

And in the light, the heat of my rage grew cold. This was a fuckin' kid. Looked like he was about twenty. I bit my lip and stared down at the ground.

"I couldn't be the guy you're looking for," he said gently. "Now could I?"

"God, man, I'm really sorry. If you knew what that fucker did to my sister, you'd understand why I'm so fuckin' mad. But it couldn't be you... Shit, you were probably still in diapers when all of this went down."

He smiled. "I'm sorry for...for whatever happened. Is it okay if I get on my way?"

"Sure, sure, go on. Again, I'm really sorry."

He started to walk away. *Stupid, stupid!* I told myself. I could have killed that guy! An innocent guy, and I could have cut him down in his prime. *God, Davio, get a grip.*

I started back to the club. Lucinda was outside, the snow falling around that sick little face.

"Why didn't you off the fucker?" she shrieked. "He deserves it." She came up to me, and I could smell her foul breath. "Man, that dude probably had some serious cash on him."

I pushed her away. "I don't kill people for money. And this guy wasn't the one I was looking for anyway. Too young."

Lucinda laughed. "Too young? Dude! Do you know how old that fucker is? He's the same age as me and you! I don't know how he does it, but he hasn't changed a bit in, God, like, twenty years."

I couldn't believe this. I turned and ran down the street. Turning the corner, all I saw was the glow of two dwindling red lights, the back of a taxi. My chance gone up in vapor, just like the exhaust coming out of the tailpipe.

"Fuck," I whispered.

There would be another chance. There had to be.

Chapter Twenty-Five

GARY

Lake Geneva sits, a beautiful Wisconsin jewel, an hour north of Chicago. Its shores, dotted with mansions bearing tribute, have been home to the wealthy for many years. The place has the feel of a Midwestern Cote d'Azur, a gathering place of the rich and famous but still retaining the feel of the apple-pie center of the United States. An improbable pairing, but a lovely one nonetheless.

It is here I find myself on a weekend retreat, not long after my encounter with Davio D'Angelo. I have come at the invitation of Beth Markham, progeny of the Markham Foods family. Markham Foods has become one of the staples of the American diet, a corporation with factories across the country, producing processed delights for the masses. Normally I think I would have not accepted the invitation, save for two factors. One, Henrietta would be there, and her charm and wit always worked like a balm on my soul; and two, I needed desperately to get away, to try to put behind me the traumatic encounter with Davio D'Angelo in that South Side alley.

Beth Markham is one of the women who have fallen for my charms, heedless of the effect it would have on her marriage—which faltered and eventually died under the weight of her obsession with me, an obsession at the time I did nothing to discourage—and her children, who, one by one, have gone to live with their father. Beth's eyes still light up whenever I enter a room, but behind them is a deadness born of disappointment. We have stayed friends since our affair ended. But there is a wariness that lies dormant between us, dormant, at least, until we are alone. Then it resurfaces, and in her eyes I can see the longing, the thwarted desire.

I feel sorry for her. She is a beautiful woman. Statuesque, I believe, is the right word. Six feet tall, with straight black hair and blue eyes, the proof of her mother's Irish heritage. She has had all the plastic surgery people have whispered I have had and still manages to retain the looks of a woman in her late twenties, when she is actually in her early forties.

Saturday evening. It's early. We have just finished dinner, and outside the sun is a dying burst of orange mixed with lavender, pink, and dark gray skies. There are ten of us, including Henrietta and Beth, wandering around the "great room," a large high-ceilinged-beamed room with one wall of glass facing the lake. Each of us holds a snifter of Courvoisier, and bearing testimony to the times and the people who feel they have to follow trends, many of us are smoking cigars...Cubans. Their sweet aroma and the ephemeral gray swirls of smoke hang in the air. Henrietta is holding court as usual, regaling the group with a story about her early days as a drag queen in Atlanta. How she, as a sixteen-year-old boy, would sneak out at night to participate in the shows and contests.

Everyone is laughing at the image of her running down Peachtree Street in four-inch spikes, trying to catch the last bus of the night. Everyone but me. I had thought that coming here might help me forget Davio D'Angelo and, worse, Zoe. The ruin I made of their lives. A cold pinprick of terror presses into my heart when I think of how close Zoe's brother came to killing me. And it depresses me to think I could inspire such hatred in another human being.

I wander away from the group, walking slowly up and down teakwood-planked floors, until I come to the Markham library. Inside, a fire has been laid, and the leather-bound volumes seem to stare at me as I enter—reproachfully, I think. They, like me, have aged well, but they owe their distinguished status to talent and intellect, whereas I owe mine to the devil. The walls here are covered with framed blow-ups of print ads that have appeared for various Markham Foods products throughout the decades—macaroni and cheese, Samson Frozen Dinners, Sweet Kisses sugar substitute—all bearing testimony in a white-trash sort of way to the Markhams, who wouldn't be caught dead putting any of this food in their mouths.

I look outside at the calm, unruffled waters of Lake Geneva. The sun has set, leaving behind it a few strands of pale pink at the horizon. The sight is almost calming, and as I puff on my cigar, I try to imagine myself in those waters, the cool liquid a cradle for me. It is a kind of meditation but one I am aware of. I take deep, slow breaths, inhaling through my nose, exhaling through my mouth, trying to filter out everything that has brought me down lately. *I can change*, I think, over and over, making of the three simple words a mantra.

And then my heart stops.

A dark figure scuttles across the great lawn spread outside. A man, hurrying, his figure almost a silhouette, backlit. All the calm evaporates, and my scalp prickles. A line of sweat forms at my hairline. I press my face to the glass, trying to see better.

The figure reaches a lightpost near the pier and turns.

"God," I gasp, and suddenly the room swirls around me in nauseating movement and everything goes black.

*

When I awaken, they are all standing over me...the entire weekend guest list. Henrietta is kneeling above me, a washcloth in her hand. She smiles when our eyes meet.

"Welcome back to Kansas, Dorothy."

I get up on one elbow, disoriented, the events of the past few moments forgotten. "What happened?"

"You tell us, honey. We just heard a thud and came running. There you were...passed out cold."

I sit up more, and Henrietta hands me a glass of water. I gulp half its contents down and look around the room until my eyes light on the big floor-to-ceiling window out of which I saw him.

Davio D'Angelo.

I look at the crowd and put on my best sheepish grin. "Too much cognac and cigar smoke, I guess." I pull on Henrietta's bejeweled hand, and she peers down at me, her eyebrows together, questioning.

"I saw a ghost," I whisper.

*

It is later, much later. The house is enveloped in silence and, for the most part, darkness. The revelers have all retired, heads swimming with liquor and laughter, to separate bedrooms with private baths...among the rich, there is no lack of privacy. I try to do the same. But every time my head hits the cool pillow, images of Davio D'Angelo swim before me, and I see him creeping in through my door, scuttling across the oriental-carpeted room like an insect, knife glinting as it catches the moonlight. My eyes burn, but there is nothing I can do to bring sleep on. I had drunk as much alcohol as the others, yet in that warm, amber-colored liquid there was no relief, no deliverance from my torment.

The path to the straight and narrow is a difficult one, uphill all the way, strewn with boulders and brambles.

I rise about three and go downstairs, thinking that if sleep won't cooperate with me, I might as well do something useful. I slide into a pair of jeans and a sweatshirt and pad downstairs. In the breakfast room, I find a recent copy of the *New Yorker* and sit down with a mug of warmed milk to read it.

It isn't long before I hear the whisper of footsteps behind me and then feel the delicate touch of feminine hands upon my shoulders. I smell patchouli and know Beth stands behind me. She kneads my shoulders.

"My," she whispers, "aren't we tense tonight?" She presses her fingertips in deep, and I have to admit her ministrations feel good, loosening the knots and steel bands tension has formed in my shoulders. "It feels like iron under there."

Beneath the patchouli, I smell alcohol borne on her soft voice. She leans down and plants a kiss on the back of my neck. It makes me shiver.

I shrug her away.

"Come upstairs with me, Gary."

I bite my lip. Is this what she has invited me here for? "I don't think so, Beth. Those days were a long time ago. They're over now."

She pouts and, even with her plastic surgery, I still can't help but think the pout would look pretty only on a much younger woman.

"There's no reason they can't begin again. You're single. I'm single." She grins. "Let's make the most of it."

I stand and take her in my arms, feeling her warmth, the firmness beneath the lace nightgown she wears. I lean down and kiss her, my tongue exploring the inside of her mouth.

She does not taste sweet. The lingering effects of alcohol and cigar have made her breath sour, and it's easy for me to pull away, to stick to my resolve. I shake my head and gently take her chin in my hand, forcing her blue eyes to meet mine. "We can't. I'm not the same man I used to be." *Oh God, let it be true.*

"Is there someone else?"

"Not yet." I cross the room to stare out at the blackness. I almost expect to be confronted with the specter of Davio D'Angelo's face, but all is still.

I listen as Beth takes down a glass from the cupboard, opens the freezer, and dumps a handful of ice in the glass. The *glug-glug* of liquid being added.

I can hear her sipping, and the wet sound makes me want to hurry from the room, to go back to the torment of another sleepless night in another luxurious bedroom.

In an instant, I hear her draining the dregs from her glass.

"I can't sleep either. Daddy just bought me a brand-new Lexus. What do you say we go for a drive? The roads are empty now."

"That sounds like a good idea." Anything would be preferable to being caught alone with her and having to resist her advances.

*

We head down a lonely country road, towering trees illuminated by the headlights as Beth takes the turns too fast, sending up gravel when she veers off the road.

"Beth... Beth, maybe you should slow down."

She giggles and presses harder on the accelerator. The sleepy landscape speeds by, and I am frightened. I know she is drunk, and I'm grateful there is no one out on this cold midweek night. Beth swerves across the double yellow line and rights the car again, giggling.

"Maybe we should head back now." I feel an odd foreboding...perhaps not so odd in light of the fact of Beth's driving, her speed and inability to keep the car in its lane. Something bad is going to happen, and I don't want to end up a traffic fatality just when I've found the road to what I hope is salvation.

"Come on, Beth, turn around. Let me drive."

"Don't be stupid. I do this all the time."

She leans over, and the car swerves across the road, floating, as she rummages in the glove compartment. Her laugh is crystalline as she pulls out a sterling silver flask and opens it, drinks. I grab the steering wheel and force her back into the lane where she belongs.

"C'mon, let me drive!" My heart beats faster now, and I'm beginning to sweat.

"Get out of here!" she slurs.

We argue, and as our voices rise, Beth rounds a blind curve, tires squealing, making her laugh...but there is no mirth in this laugh, only vindictiveness, as if she is punishing me. I struggle for the wheel as the dread rises up in me, the certainty that we will come to rest only when the car collides with something. Her laughter, the quickening thump of my heart, and the screeching of tires on damp pavement seem to coalesce, rising in a terrifying crescendo. This is all happening so fast!

A figure stands poised at the edge of the road. Just as our headlights pick out the dark form, it makes a dash. Beth gasps and jerks the steering wheel...the wrong way. Instead of pointing the car out of harm's way, it's as if she's aiming directly for the person in the road, a dark shape hurtling in front of us. A man, but even with his speed, he is moving too slow, too slow. I brace myself and whimper "No" as he looms large before us. There is a thud, and then he is up on the hood, then flying off. His body slams against the windshield as he slides across the hood, the impact leaving a spiderweb crack and a smear of blood.

"Oh God! Oh God!" I scream, and Beth slams on the brakes. We skid and come to rest at the side of the road. I look back and see someone lying on the road...a dark figure, a man. That's all I can discern in the darkness. He's not moving. I'm afraid I will vomit.

I start to open my door. Beth grabs my arm. "No!" she shrieks. "Do you realize the kind of trouble I could get into?"

"Are you crazy? He could die."

She clings to me, holding fast, with a strength born of the adrenaline I can smell in her sweat, the hot, sour tang.

"I can't have a scandal. Please, Gary." Her eyes are glistening with tears. She speaks all in a rush. "If I get mixed up in this, Blake won't let me see the children. I can't lose my children!"

She grabs my face, the nails digging in, painful.

"We'll go right home. Better, there's a pay phone up around the bend at the store... We can call an ambulance. Please, Gary, please..."

Her despair causes a wave of emotions to play tug of war in my heart, in my brain. Stupidly, I give in. I turn and look at the lump lying on the road as Beth, careful now, puts the car in drive and starts heading away. Please, please don't let another car come along.

Finally I do roll down the window and vomit, sick of myself more than anything else.

*

Morning comes with a dull gray sheen. The waters of Lake Geneva are gray, the sky a dull bluish-white. The lack of color seems fitting when I awaken about 10:00 a.m. after a few restless hours of sleep, hours in which I was unable to stop the endless brain loop of the man in the road, caught in the headlights of Beth's Lexus. I try everything to rid my mind of the image, but it keeps returning with a power of its own, unrelenting, almost as if its appearance in my mind's eye is beyond my control.

I sit up in bed. The others are below me, voices filtering dully up the stairs, and I envy their innocence... trying to recall how it felt to be a person who had never caused another's death.

Last night, I think, was an omen, and it frightens me, makes my resolve stronger.

There is a tap on my door, and I call, "Come on in." Henrietta enters, wearing a long pale blue dress. These days, she has been favoring a black wig with long dreadlocks. I stifle a grim giggle; she looks like Whoopi Goldberg. I tremble with the laughter inside. It owes more to hysteria than to mirth. She doesn't notice my struggle to hold back the laughter, not knowing that to give into it might set me to screaming.

After crossing the room, she sits on the edge of the bed. "Beth told me what happened last night."

"It was horrible." I reach over to the nightstand, shake a cigarette out, and light it. I blow the smoke toward the ceiling. "Has anyone heard anything?"

Henrietta shakes her head. "Not yet, but I'm sure in a place this small, it won't be long."

I stare down at the sheets covering me, sit up more firmly against the pillows. "What happened last night... It means something."

Henrietta cocks her head. "What, Gary, could it possibly mean? Do you think that accidents are set out by God to have some secret message for you alone?"

I shake my head, knowing Henrietta finds me egotistical, and I suppose she's right. "I take it as a message anyway, a warning."

"A warning about what, dear?"

"That my life is shit. That I better wake up to that fact."

She grasps my hand. "Gary...no one has a better life than you. There is no one who wouldn't be delighted to change places with you."

I don't know what to say. Who would want this miserable, secretive, lonely existence? It just goes to show how the world is caught up only in the surface of things and not what lies beneath.

All at once, the image comes before me again, and I look, wide-eyed, at Henrietta. I begin to cry, and I rub my hands angrily against my eyes, trying to dam the flow of tears. "I'm afraid, Henrietta."

"Of what? What do you have to be afraid of? Lord knows you've got everything."

"Death." I gaze toward the window. "It's waiting for me. Outside. I can see it."

She turns and looks toward the window, as if some grinning black rictus might be there, pressed against the panes.

There is a gentle rapping at the door, and before I can say anything, Beth comes into the room. Her long black hair is loose against another long white nightgown, similar to the one she wore last night. I wonder if she has a closet full of them, or if this is the same one she had on when she mowed down that poor man in the road.

"There's news." Her lips tremble, and I notice then how tired her eyes look, red-rimmed and puffy. "He's dead."

"How do you know?"

"It was on the radio this morning."

I reach over toward the chair on the side of the bed, where my jacket is slung across its back. I fumble inside the pocket for my checkbook. "I want to give the family something. I can at least help with funeral expenses."

"He didn't have any family," Beth says dully. "No one up here even seems to know him or what he was doing up here."

Dread begins to trickle into my bloodstream. I know what she is about to say before she says it, and my mouth goes dry. "Who was it? Did they say?"

"A guy on leave from the Army."

I shiver.

"His name was Davio D'Angelo."

I slump against the pillows, heart thudding so loud I feel both Henrietta and Beth must be able to hear it. I drop the checkbook on the floor and lean back against the pillows, close my eyes. A wave of nausea passes through me, and I can't deny it, the sick feeling is mixed with relief.

Beth gets up and leaves the room, saying nothing more.

Henrietta and I sit silently for a while. I sigh. "I wish I could just escape."

"Escape from what, honey? Your life? There's only one escape hatch, and Miss Henrietta isn't about to let her best friend go that route."

I clutch her hand. "Don't you see? We murdered him!"

"It was an accident, that's all. Beth may have been drunk and stupid, just like she always is, but it was an accident." Henrietta regards her nails and smiles. "I'd like to know someone who committed a real murder."

I close my eyes again, thinking but not saying *You already do.*

Chapter Twenty-Six

HENRIETTA

You would think that boy would have learned his lesson. But oh no, there we were, headed back to Chicago down Route 41, and Gary was tearing through the curves like he was farther east, in Indianapolis. I giggled and fired up a cheroot. "Honey, you better slow down, you know what's good for you." His eyes never seemed to leave the road, not even to give me one of his shocked stares. As if Miss Henrietta could ever let a sensible, pedestrian word pass her red-lacquered lips.

I clicked my seat belt into place and decided if it was my time to go, then it was my time to go. The landscape, what I could see of it rushing by, was beautiful, the sun slanting down all golden, like you get in late afternoon. The road was lined with trees and just occasionally marred by the sight of a billboard or a car dealership.

We stopped at one of the few lights on this route, and it was there that Gary finally decided to break the silence.

"I should have done the right thing years ago. If I had just gone on and married Zoe D'Angelo instead of being such a stupid shit, things would have been different for me. I know it."

I rolled my eyes. "Honey, what are you talking about? There is no right thing. If there's one thing I've learned, it's that. People who think different are just slow or stupid. They bore me." I regarded my fingernails, seeing that they needed a touch-up. "And there ain't nothin' in this world worse than boredom."

"Oh yes, Henrietta, there is."

I have to be honest; this boy was beginning to bore *me*. I wondered when this somber routine was going to end. I mean, what happened up at the lake with this Davio D'Angelo character was terrible, but hell, accidents happened every day, to good people and bad, and truth be told, this guy didn't have much going on. From what I heard, they couldn't even find anyone to notify that the guy was dead. So...he would not be missed...and as for him, well, he doesn't know any different, does he? Death is wonderful for wiping out one's sorrows. Not to mention the potential for sheer drama...

"Okay, Gary, what's worse than boredom? I mean, honestly."

"Corruption. And I'm not talking about Chicago politics here." He made a halfhearted attempt at a grin, knowing his little joke cut a tad too close to the bone for me. I, who had just been dumped by one of Chicago's first openly gay judges. He was afraid of what I might do to his career. We'd see what a weeping widow like me would do to his career...but enough about me.

"I'm talking about..." Gary's voice trailed off as he stared out the window. The trees were becoming fewer as we got closer and closer to the city. "I'm talking about corruption of the soul, the kind that eats away at your spirit, at your heart."

"Oh Lord, a philosopher."

He took his eyes off the road for a moment to regard me. "Can you be serious for once in your life?"

Good thing the boy didn't give me a chance to reply.

"I mean moral corrosion, the kind that comes from...well, the kind that comes from the type of life I've led...the drugs, the anonymous sex, the drinking, the seducing...and don't be glib, like that's some kind of high life. It's not. It's empty, and I'm sick of it."

We drove on in silence. I didn't know what to tell him. I didn't think he was in the mood to hear that just about everyone I knew would give their left tit or nut to trade places with him. The fun ones, anyway. The ones who whispered behind his back about him were life's worst offenders. The dullards. Boring. Most of them hypocrites anyway.

"I didn't tell you about Amber."

He left an open space hanging in the car, waiting for me to bite. Tiredly, "Who's Amber?" I asked, shuddering at the name. It sounded like one of the gals down at the Façade. I remembered one called Forever Amber. Shit.

"Are you listening, Henrietta? I met Amber not long before we went up to the lake. We had a wonderful week together. She wasn't a city girl. Lived up in Woodstock where, thankfully, no one knew me."

"Woodstock, huh? Where they roll up the sidewalks at ten and all the lights are on blinkers by eleven?"

Gary blew out a big sigh. I could tell I was working his last nerve, so I shut up.

"She was beautiful...untouched, you know."

"Hadn't enjoyed the embraces of men or barnyard animals?"

Gary ignored me. "It's been a long time since I've seen someone so young, you know. Someone whose eyes were clear... She had the smoothest skin I've ever touched...like a baby's. Long blonde hair, blue eyes. Came from a nice family... Her father owned a little video store, and her mother did crafts that she sold at fairs. Nice people. Good people."

"What's the point?"

"The point is we fell in love. And we had five blissful days together...walking in the woods, holding hands, a kiss now and then, nothing more."

"What did you say her name was again? Rebecca? Of Sunny-fuckin'-brook Farm?" I blew out a sigh, wishing I could just get the fuck out of this car! "So what's the problem?"

Gary smiled, but there was something sad in his eyes. "I want to be good, Henrietta, so I did something selfless to prove to myself that I could."

"So you didn't fuck her. What is this, a first?"

Gary shook his head. "I left her, Henrietta. I knew I could probably bring nothing good into her life, and even though it broke my heart, I told her I couldn't see her anymore. I did a *good* thing. Don't you see that?"

"How delicious, honey. You broke her heart."

"You miss the point. I did a good thing...a selfless thing. For the first time in a long, long time, I put someone else's well-being before my own."

"Well, bully for you. Bully! I'm sure that Miss Amber might beg to differ."

"Amber didn't hold all the cards. She didn't know my past. She didn't know about Zoe D'Angelo and about how I passed the hours down in Chicago. If she had, she too would have seen that she was better off without me."

We stopped at another light, and Gary turned to regard me. "This is the beginning for me, Henrietta. I'm changed. I'm going to be good... You'll see."

"Well, I wish you all the best. I really do. You'll be the only person I know who considers himself good. The scandals just seem to keep growing in the city of big shoulders. There's some new corruption, as you like to call it, every day. Have you heard the latest on Liam?"

The light changed, and Gary floored the BMW. I saw his ruddy glow vanish when I mentioned Liam.

"What do you mean?"

"Last I heard, they were saying that Liam never turned up in New York when he was supposed to. Nobody seems to be able to find him. We both know Liam, Gary, and we both know that him doing something like just disappearing is simply out of the question. If nothing else, he was reliable."

"So what's up now?"

There was a stiffness to his voice, and I wondered if the fact that Liam was missing was the only thing giving him the jitters.

"The police are looking into it. As they say in the papers, foul play is suspected."

Gary didn't say anything for a while, just drove on, faster than before. We would be at my apartment within the hour.

I had just about thought we would finish the ride in silence when, near the exit ramp for Addison, Gary said, in a soft voice, "What would you say if I told you I killed Liam?"

I snorted. "Honey, I would say you don't have the balls for such a dramatic display." I shook my head. "It just isn't in you."

Gary didn't say anything to that. But it was the truth. Gary may have learned how to party over the years, and he was an incorrigible slut and had a head for drugs, but there was just no fucking way someone like him could kill anyone, least of all Liam.

"I hope Liam's all right," I said, ignoring the turn the conversation was taking. I was worried about the man... Something not right was definitely up, but thinking that Gary had anything to do with that was simply out of the question. I refused to believe, though, that Liam was dead.

"It's weird, you know. Him disappearing like this, right when he's at the top of his game."

I laughed. "Top of his game. Honey, I don't really think he's been at the top of his game for the last ten years. His work had lost all its fire. But that's the way it goes in this country."

"What do you mean?"

"Commercial success. Pap for the masses. Liam had lowered himself to the lowest common denominator. To what sells. I guess in this great country of ours, that's what makes somebody a success. A mixture of good intentions and bad art." I stared out the window as Gary flew off the exit ramp onto Ohio Street. "I refuse to believe Liam's dead." I gave a short little laugh, but truth be told, I was no longer in a humorous mood. "You know, honey, the one thing that scares Miss Henrietta absolutely out of her wits is death."

Gary laughed as we headed into downtown. "I didn't think anything scared you. I thought you were above all that."

"Well, we all have our fears."

"I wish I had never posed for him."

"What?"

"I wish I had never sat for him. It changed everything."

I knew, on some weird gut level, what he meant. Since the day Liam began working on that hologram, everything changed. Gary was nowhere near the boy I met in Liam's studio that fine summer day so many years ago. Even if his face hadn't changed. Even if his body didn't show the settling most men of his age were prone to. I was just about to ask him what was up with that, to finally give the goods to Miss Henrietta, when he spoke again.

"I've been doing a lot of rereading, you know, the classics of my youth. There's a line from Hamlet, I think, that sums things up for me. It goes:

Like the painting of a sorrow,
A face without a heart."

Dusk was approaching, and I suddenly felt very weary. I had grown up Southern Baptist, and try as I might to rinse *that* stain out, I could never shake the Bible study I had had to do as a child, and I said simply, "What does it profit a man if he gains the whole world and loses his own soul?"

Gary pulled the car over to the curb. I noticed his hands were trembling on the steering wheel. Weakly, I made a joke. "What, you think if I quote from the Bible, the car's going to go up in flames?"

There was an intensity in his aqua eyes as he stared at me. I do believe it looked a little like shock.

"Why would you ask me that?"

I shrugged it off and let go of it. "Oh, who knows? I heard it from one of those assholes who preach from the sidewalk downtown."

"Don't make light of the soul." He pulled back into traffic and stared rigidly forward. "The soul is a terrible reality. That's something I feel very, very strongly about, Henrietta. It's the truth."

"Ah, there's no such thing as a soul, honey." Even I didn't believe my words. "The things one feels strongly about are never true." We were almost to Lake Shore

Drive. Home. Empty. But hey, this girl has never wanted for admirers. I pulled down the sun visor and caught my reflection. Crow's-feet and laugh lines... Once upon a time, the makeup could hide them. Now I needed spackle. "Gary, honey, I gotta tell you, I'm glad to be getting out of this car. You have just become too serious, I swear. You have nothing to worry about. You've held on to your youth, and that's all that counts."

He pulled to the curb, popped the trunk. "I mean it, Henrietta, even if it's boring to you. From now on, I am a changed man. No more drugs, no more anonymous sex, no buying binges at Neiman Marcus."

"Yeah, yeah, right." I swung my legs from the seat. "I suppose dinner tomorrow night is out of the question."

Gary smiled at me. The first time, I think, on this long, god-awful ride.

"Just no clubs afterward."

I nodded and got out of the car.

"Henrietta..."

I looked back. His mouth was poised to say something, but then his features softened, as if he had changed his mind. I didn't pursue what it was he was about to say.

Chapter Twenty-Seven

GARY

It's still early evening and unseasonably warm. I decide, since it's only a mile or so, to walk home after dinner with Henrietta. The traffic swarms by on the Inner Drive... *All these lives*, I think, *all on their way to homes, families*. And me to my *Architectural Digest* home, with no one to share all my beautiful things. All this collecting I've done: art and antiques—the best of everything!—and it might as well be in a warehouse for all it's appreciated.

I pass a couple of people I know, people I've partied with in clubs and at after-hours parties, and neither of them say hello. Their eyes are cast downward, as if they don't see me, as if the sidewalk holds something fascinating. In spite of my wholesome, healthy good looks, I have become a grim reminder of debauchery and excess. Oh well, all of that is about to change. I will have new friends and a new lover...someone more than that, really. I can be a good man; I know it. And the hologram—I see the lurid thing in my mind's eye: monstrous, yellow eyes and lesions, wasting, blood staining its hands, a crippled face—will revert back, reflecting the light with which I plan to fill my life from this day forward.

No more darkness.

As if in counterpoint to the dark horror of the hologram, I suddenly see Amber in my mind. We sit on the porch at the back of her family's house, on a wooden swing suspended from the ceiling. The night is cool, and our bodies touch, a comforting warmth, as we swing back and forth, lulling...no need for words. Beyond us, the day's light fades, the sun's golden light washing everything, the expanse of yard and the stand of pines, ash, and maples of the woods beyond, with a bath of yellow.

"You're so funny," she whispers, snuggling her head into my shoulder, and I can't recall, for anything, what I had said to prompt her remark.

But I remember the feel of her warmth against me, the pleasant weight of her head on my shoulder. I can still feel her silken hair as I ran my fingers through it. The easy rise and fall of her breathing as we sat, content, on that back porch.

She didn't know that later that night, I would tell her goodbye. Didn't know how her eyes were yet to fill with tears, how sharply she would intake her breath, as if I had stabbed her, my words powerful enough to wound with real pain.

I pause outside my building and wonder what I'm doing. Is it really possible, now, to become good? Am I delusional? Can anything ever really be reversed?

Amber, running up the stairs of the front hall of her family home, leaving the door ajar, stung with the pain of rejection, never knowing I did it for her own good.

Or did I? Did I really? The darkness descends on me, both inward and outward. I feel trapped...trapped in a web I've woven myself, wanting things that cost a terrible price. Was hurting Amber really a good thing? Was it really so selfless? Or was it the supreme act of selfishness? Hurting someone else so I could delude myself into believing I was sparing her? Sacrificing my life so another might live? I bark out a short, bitter laugh, causing an old man, a newspaper tucked under his arm, to stare. He really isn't so old, I think, as he hurries by in his trench coat. Hell, he could be my own age and he would never guess, looking at me, that we were contemporaries.

I move through the revolving doors, barely acknowledging the greeting the doorman calls out. All I want to do is get upstairs and perhaps never come out again.

The elevator stands, door open like a dark maw, waiting to swallow. "So serious, Gary!" I hear Henrietta chide, laughing. I get in and press one of the top buttons to take me to this home in which I've barricaded myself...a place filled with mirrors that once reflected the delight I found in my own image.

I take out my keys as I head down the corridor. They jingle, too loud, in the lush, insulated silence of the building. The mirror threw back, I understood now, a falsehood. The only time it was true was seventeen, eighteen years ago. The rest of the time, it has been a sham.

Inside, I draw a glass of water from the kitchen tap and go to the living room, where I sip, staring out at the smooth, gray façade of the lake, which will vanish along with the ambient light of dusk. I see the boy I once was, and even though I look no different now, that boy is as far from me as my soul is far from God.

I miss him. Oh God, do I miss him. Most people retain a small part of the child within them, even as they wither and wrinkle, but I have thrown away my soul to avoid the aging, and only now do I realize what a ransom I have paid...

The realization, the truth of the matter...that I really did give my soul, stares back at me in the window's glass.

There behind me, in the glass, Zoe D'Angelo appears. She wears an oversized T-shirt and a leotard. Her long dark hair falls gracefully over her shoulders, and her eyes bore into mine. She knows I am watching her. Hands poised above her head, she twirls, a pirouette. Spinning faster, faster, until she becomes a blur.

She stops. And I see that her face is ruined. Chemical burns stain her beauty. Her neck lolls, making of her a rag doll.

I close my eyes, biting my lower lip until I taste the coppery warmth of my own blood. When I open them again, it is only my own reflection I see in the glass.

I finish my water, watching the light fade from gray to dark, standing there motionless, not thinking, for God knows how long.

The apartment is silent, and I feel as if this silence entraps me. Even though the trees tell a tale of high winds, I cannot hear the shriek of the cool air as it rushes across the surface of the lake, nor can I hear the waves crashing against the boulders so far below. I am insulated. Cut off.

I wander away from the glass, and as I pass through the living room, I pass a large mirror, framed in wood, after the style of Chippendale. My heart thuds as I see, behind my own image, that of Andy Crause, my cohort in the disposal of Liam's corpse. White hands reach out, grasping. He looks far too pale, and I notice the dark hole in the center of his forehead, the ragged flesh surrounding it, the smudge of powder burn encircling its darkness. Does this mean I am responsible for his suicide? The gunshot to the head not long after he assisted me?

I turn from the mirror but can't help looking back one final time, to make sure his soul hasn't somehow gotten trapped in the wood-framed glass.

It isn't until much later that night, after the obliviating effects of scotch and Valium, that I see the third image, in the bathroom's medicine cabinet mirror. This time there is no fright when the wraith appears behind me as I brush my teeth. It is who I expect, Davio D'Angelo. His smile is filled with malice, but I know soon the smile will fade away, to be replaced by openmouthed horror, a scream lit up by headlights. I do not wait for the transformation. Instead I click off the bathroom light and head down the hall to my bedroom.

"No!" I scream when I enter the room. There, in the freestanding mirror in the corner of the room is the image of Liam. He appears in the pose of so many cheap homages to Christ, except instead of a robe, he holds his crisp white shirt open to reveal a ravaged heart. A single drop of crimson slides from the corner of his mouth.

I dash back to the bathroom, where I cling to cool ceramic walls as what I've eaten this night comes back up in a volcano of bile and acid, leaving me weak and gasping, eyes tearing.

After a while my breathing returns to normal, and I splash cold water on my face, rinse the taste of vomit from my mouth.

I close my eyes in the darkness of the bathroom, sitting on the toilet, my throbbing head resting against the cool porcelain of the sink. I don't know how long I sit here, waiting, waiting for something to come. I don't know what. Inspiration, perhaps. An epiphany?

But after a long time, nothing happens. I realize that the course of my life, now taken, must remain true. I must do whatever I can to lead a life free of reproach. Moral. Good. Kind.

My body feels heavy, and my eyes burn. I can't go back to my bedroom. I don't know that I ever can. Perhaps it would be best to get out of this place, sell off the expensive things, and live a simpler life. It's good to have a plan, and tomorrow I will begin the dismantling of my decadent lifestyle.

I wander into my bedroom, sit on the bed. Even though I am so tired I feel I can barely move, I know that when my head touches the pillow, I will be able to do nothing but stare at the ceiling, mind racing.

I pick up the phone, hit the speed dial, and listen to the distant chirping of Henrietta's phone. I don't know why I'm calling, and before I have a chance to formulate a reason, she picks up.

"Hello?"

I bite my lip and quickly replace the receiver in its cradle. Seconds later the phone rings, startling me. I know it's Henrietta, her caller ID letting her know I was that evening's "prank" call. I let the phone ring until the voice mail picks it up. I close my eyes, breathe in deeply, and all it once, it comes to me...the epiphany I've been waiting for all evening.

New energy infuses me as I rise from the bed. I wonder why I haven't thought of this before. Of course, this is the right action!

I slip into a pair of Nikes and grab my keys. The elevator has been waiting all evening, as if it had known I would come to this decision and would need to be spirited as quickly as possible down to the basement storage room.

As I descend, I feel better than I have in a long time. The course of action before me is so simple, so easy. I'm amazed I haven't done this years ago.

But years ago I wasn't ready, and maybe being ready, at last, is what allowed the idea to come to me.

On the first floor, I switch elevators, pull the metal grate of the freight elevator across, and press the *B* button. Creaking and vibrating, the elevator makes its way down.

The basement is dark, lit dimly by a few hanging bulbs. I wish I didn't have to look at the hologram again. My footsteps echo on the concrete floor. I make a turn and pause in front of the door to my storage room. My key is in my hand, but something holds me back.

No. I have to be strong. This will be the first step in my salvation, the reclaiming of my soul.

I thrust the key into the lock and swing the door open. I think I hear something scuttle through the darkness. Imagination... It has to be. I reach for the light switch and flood the room with buzzing fluorescent light.

The hologram, shrouded in purple, waits. The bright color makes it the first thing to which my eye is drawn.

The other thing my gaze falls upon is the mallet. What would my grandfather have thought if some seer had told him his grandson would one day use it to murder?

I pick up the mallet, feeling its heft. Fitting...that the mallet that killed Liam, the creator of the vehicle that brought me to this wretched place in life, should now be used to put an end to it. A full circle.

I lift the shroud and gasp. The hologram always has the power to shock, no matter how many times I see it. A demon stares back. My hair has fallen out, and the wasting that has taken place on the body leaves a face that is almost skeletal, bones pressing against thin, lesioned flesh...a grinning death rictus. The eyes are ringed in darkness, the whites dirty and red-veined. The body is the true horror, though, covered in dark lesions...their raised surfaces so real they repel me, as if I can feel their roughness beneath my fingertips. I'm so thin in this pale vision of light that my stomach is concave, the ribs obvious, forming a protective ring around my innards. And the only color the crimson that drips from my hands.

I breathe in deeply. This is the only way.

I raise the mallet high.

Chapter Twenty-Eight

HENRIETTA

This was for real; you know what I'm saying? This fear, this anxiety, completely unfounded by anything other than emotion, was as real as the concrete beneath my feet as I jumped from the cab and hurried down Lake Shore Drive to Gary's building. My heart was pounding; it was hard to breathe. Not from the running but from the anxiety that had been overpowering me since Gary called and hung up.

Something terrible had happened. Could feel it in my fuckin' bones. As if to confirm this, an ambulance swung up, red lights twirling.

Oh God, please no...

I have lost too many friends already. Not him, not my Gary...

Already a crowd of onlookers had gathered, their faces lit up alternately by the whirling red lights of the ambulance.

"Let me through!" I screamed, pushing people out of my way. "Let me through."

A policeman stopped me at the door. "Are you a resident, ma'am?"

"No, but I think something's happened to my friend."

"Who's your friend?"

"Gary Adrion."

"Give me a sec." The officer left me standing there, trying to decide if I should just bolt for the elevator. I watched as he talked to a man who was all too obviously a detective. The detective, burly, dressed bad in a plaid wool sport coat and dark slacks, a cigar clamped between his teeth, approached me. His red hair had been combed over a bald spot. I loved that in a man!

"You know Gary Adrion?"

I bit my lip and nodded. For once in my life, I couldn't find my voice. "What's happened?" I managed to whisper.

"A body was discovered a little while ago in Mr. Adrion's storage room."

"Is it him?"

"No, no, we're not sure who it is. But if you're close to Mr. Adrion, perhaps you could help us make a preliminary identification. Do you think you could do that? Do you know Mr. Adrion well?"

This was all happening too fast for an old girl like me. My head was swimming. A body found in Gary's storage room? What was that all about?

"I'll take a look, Detective."

I was trembling as we took the creaking and clanking freight elevator to the basement...myself, the detective, who said his name was Grubb, a paramedic, and two uniformed officers.

I suddenly didn't want to go through with this. But it was too late to turn back. *One foot in front of the other, Henrietta, one foot in front of the other...*

The door yawned open, a rectangle of yellow light spilling out into the corridor. My stomach felt like it had lodged in my throat. Something horrible was waiting.

"Can I just go ahead and take a look by myself?" I said to Grubb, who nodded and held out his hand to hold the others back.

I moved toward the light, feeling a little dizzy. I stumbled once and turned back to grin stupidly.

Henrietta, you've never been a baby. You may be a big old drag queen, but you're no sissy. Now get your ass in gear!

I hurried, determination making me grit my teeth, to the open doorway, propelling myself with will power, forcing myself to look with the same force.

At first I didn't know what was going on. The glass dome that had once held Liam's hologram of Gary was shattered. Shards of glass littered the gritty concrete floor. But on the marble platform, Gary still stood, the dim pinkish glow of the holographic light revealing the masterpiece, showcasing Gary's beauty in a magnificent way...a true work of art.

But who was this old man lying on the floor? Who was this hideous thing with the wisps of dry hair and, oh God, the lesions covering his body? He was skeletal, and his chest had collapsed. An old mallet had pierced through the skin and muscle—what was left of it, anyway. A putrid stench rolled out of the opening in the old man's chest, and I swear, I could see a bit of blackened lung within, a gray heart, smashed. I turned to gag, hand to my mouth, then realized I had seen the clothes before...and the earring, the damn earring. A diamond and sapphire stud I had given him for his birthday only last year.

This was too much. "Oh, Gary," I whispered, dropping to my knees, my trembling hand reaching out to touch skin that felt like parchment, the raised purple lesions unavoidable.

I began to scream, and scream, and scream.

Acknowledgements

I'd like to extend my gratitude to the following people for helping to make my take on Oscar Wilde's *The Picture of Dorian Gray* become a reality. To Oscar Wilde, of course, for giving me so much to think about and for being an inspiration I can only hope to aspire to. To Lori Perkins, esteemed literary agent, for first bringing to my attention the possibilities of this concept; to Thomas Strauch of Design Image Group, who published the book in its first edition and stood steadfastly behind it.

About the Author

Real Men. True Love.

Rick R. Reed is an award-winning and bestselling author of more than fifty works of published fiction. He is a Lambda Literary Award finalist. *Entertainment Weekly* has described his work as "heartrending and sensitive." *Lambda Literary* has called him: "A writer that doesn't disappoint..." Find him at www.rickrreedreality.blogspot.com. Rick lives in Palm Springs, CA, with his husband, Bruce, and their fierce Chihuahua/Shiba Inu mix, Kodi.

Email: rickrreedbooks@gmail.com

Facebook: www.facebook.com/rickrreedbooks

Twitter: @rickrreed

Website: www.rickrreedreality.blogspot.com

Other NineStar books by this author

Unraveling
Sky Full of Mysteries
The Perils of Intimacy
IM
Chaser
Raining Men
Blue Umbrella Sky
Third Eye
Legally Wed
Hungry for Love
Big Love

Out Now from Rick R. Reed

Third Eye

Who knew that a summer thunderstorm and a lost little boy would conspire to change single dad Cayce D'Amico's life in an instant? With Luke missing, Cayce ventures into the woods near their house to find his son, only to have lightning strike a tree near him, sending a branch down on his head. When he awakens the next day in the hospital, he discovers he has been blessed or cursed—he isn't sure which—with psychic ability. Along with unfathomable glimpses into the lives of those around him, he's getting visions of a missing teenage girl.

When a second girl disappears soon after the first, Cayce realizes his visions are leading him to their grisly fates. Cayce wants to help, but no one believes him. The police are suspicious. The press wants to exploit him. And the girls' parents have mixed feelings about the young man with the "third eye."

Cayce turns to local reporter Dave Newton and, while searching for clues to the string of disappearances and possible murders, a spark ignites between them. Little do they know that nearby, another couple—dark and murderous—are plotting more crimes and wondering how to silence the man who knows too much about them.

IM

One by one, he's killing them. Lurking in the digital underworld of Men4HookUpNow.com, he lures, seduces, charms, reaching out through instant messages to the unwary. They invite him over. He's just another trick. Harmless. They're dead wrong.

When the first bloody body surfaces, openly gay Chicago Police Department detective Ed Comparetto is called in to investigate. Sickened by the butchered mess of one of his brothers left on display in a bathtub, he seeks relief outside where the young man who discovered the body waits to tell him the story of how he found his friend. But who is this witness...and did he play a bigger part in the murder than he's letting on?

Comparetto is on a journey to discover the truth, a truth that he needs to discover before he loses his career, his boyfriend, his sanity...his life. Because in this killer's world, IM doesn't stand for instant message...it stands for instant murder.

Also Available from NineStar Press

Connect with NineStar Press

www.ninestarpress.com

www.facebook.com/ninestarpress

www.facebook.com/groups/NineStarNiche

www.twitter.com/ninestarpress